"Move and you're

Twenty feet up, the rock leveled off on one side, extending over the gorge. Before climbing higher, Carl Lyons decided to follow the formation to a point where he could determine if Bedson had taken a pathway down into the valley. As he approached the precipice, Lyons heard a noise off to his right, and the Able Team warrior instinctively sprang to one side. He heard the dull crack of muffled gunfire as a bullet ricocheted off the rock just behind him, stinging him with shrapnel.

An unexpected dip in the rock's surface caught Lyons off guard, and he fell, turning his ankle. Jolts of pain shot up his leg. His assailant was scrambling across the ledge toward him, but there was little he could do to protect himself. Before he could even reach for his .45, Bedson was standing over him with his own gun pressed against the Ironman's skull.

"Able Team will go anywhere, do anything, in order to complete their mission."
—*West Coast Review of Books*

Mack Bolan's

ABLE TEAM®

ABLE TEAM.

Dead Zone

Dick Stivers

A GOLD EAGLE BOOK FROM

WORLDWIDE.

TORONTO • NEW YORK • LONDON • PARIS
AMSTERDAM • STOCKHOLM • HAMBURG
ATHENS • MILAN • TOKYO • SYDNEY

First edition June 1989

ISBN 0-373-61242-7

Special thanks and acknowledgment to
Ron Renauld for his contribution to this work.

PROLOGUE

Rayford's Creek glinted from the play of sunshine on its gurgling waters. But to the trove of tourists who had paid their five dollars for a prospector's pan and an hour with which to use it, every sparkle in the stream held forth the promise of some long-elusive nugget that would bring them a small fortune. At the very least they were gaining a taste of the fever that had drawn their predecessors to the Colorado hinterland the previous century.

"Remember, now," Bones Callahan howled to the visitors through the sandy wisps of his flowing moustache, "besides the gold still sittin' in that streambed thanks to Mother Nature, there's a nugget worth three thousand dollars that we stuck in there just last week. Find that sucker and you'll be the envy of all Teller County!"

"All right!" a few children squealed in unison as they led the charge to the water's edge and began scooping the sediment with their shallow pans. Older tourists approached the creek more slowly, strategically scanning the bends and turns with a thoughtful eye, looking for the spot that showed the most promise.

The local inhabitants of Rayford's Creek were in the throes of celebrating the one hundredth anniversary of the gold find that had transformed that part of Colorado into a string of seething boomtowns that would go on to yield more than half a billion dollars worth of gold ore. The Rayford's Creek Chamber of Commerce, never one to balk at a chance to compete for the Denver tourist dollar, had joined its legendary neighbor, Cripple Creek, in a year-long festival. Their particular section of waterway was just one of a half-dozen sites in the area where, for a small admission fee, one could step back into yesteryear and experience gold-rush fever.

Bones Callahan worked part-time as one of several resident prospectors at the Rayford's Creek Gold Rush Daze exhibit. He looked the part; Bones was a physically fit man of sixty-three with the sun-bronzed skin and wild whiskers associated with the panners of old. He enjoyed spending his days in dungarees and cowboy boots, showing folks the proper technique for jostling the broad pan to separate pebbles and silt from the glimmering flakes or nuggets of gold still found in the creek after all these years. Bones had moved to Colorado eighteen years earlier from Southern California, and had immediately read all the available literature on the area's gold-mining lore. He could spin different tales to each group of tourists that visited the exhibit on any particular day. He was a popular figure at the site and was constantly being asked to work full time. But Bones held his ground in each instance, jealously guarding his free time, which he declared was set aside for some "real" prospecting up in the surrounding hills, off the beaten track and away from the more frequently visited haunts.

When his shift ended at one that afternoon, Bones wandered away from the amateurs crowding the stream and walked up the slope to the restored section of the Old West town, where fast-food stands, convenience stores and souvenir shops peddled their wares behind weathered facades. He nodded to a few arriving tourists and exchanged words with some of the other employees, who also wore period costumes. The jail at the end of the unpaved street was, in fact, the employees' lounge, and after stepping inside to gather a few things from his locker, Bones crossed the street to the small petting zoo, where he was allowed to keep his pack mule, Stubborn. The zoo's main animal handler, a woman half his age, smiled at Bones as he loaded his prospecting gear onto the mule's back.

"You never give up, do you, Bones?"

"That's right, Emily." He looked over her shoulder and up at the steep rise of Mount Paulsen in the distance. "Somewhere up there's a claim with my name on it, and I damn well intend to find it."

"Goin' on eight months now you've been sayin' that," Emily scoffed good-naturedly.

"Be sayin' it another seven if that's what it takes."

"Well, good luck to you, then."

"Is there any other kind?" Bones chuckled.

"I won't answer that," Emily said, stroking the coarse hair of a goat munching from the feed trough next to her. "Say, Bones, didn't you say your niece was coming by this afternoon?"

Bones nodded as he untethered his mule and a tawny riding horse from the hitching post. "Four o'clock. I'll be back by then. If I'm a little late, just have her wait, okay?"

"Sure thing."

Mounting the horse, Bones urged Stubborn alongside him with a gentle tug on the mule's reins. He headed away from the throng of tourists toward an old wooden bridge that spanned Rayford's Creek and brought him to a narrow dirt trail that wound up into the foothills.

"Let's just see if we can't have a better go of things today," he mumbled under his breath as he started up the gentle slope.

A proliferation of hearty aspens and tall pines veiled the rise in vibrant greens, and even the lower shrubs were thick and lush where they fed off the water of downhill streams. In less than a half hour Bones was far from view of those below, making his way through the rugged hill country. Except for the occasional far-off drone of a jet, there was no other encroachment from the twentieth century and Bones felt a peaceful contentment settle over him. The steady clopping of hooves on the dirt trail was lulling and comfortable, and the chirp of birds off in the brush or the screech of hawks circling against the dark blue sky overhead sounded almost musical.

Back during the height of the gold rush, and to some extent even recently, these and other Rocky Mountain locales had been honeycombed with deep, penetrating mines, where laborers would scrape away at the belly of hard rock in search of a rich vein of gold or other valuable ore. It was widely acknowledged that despite the tens of thousands of prospectors who had worked the territory so many years ago, there still lay untapped veins and motherlodes, just waiting to be discovered. It was the prospect of such a discovery that motivated Bones's frequent excursions into the mountains, and the occasional nugget or flakes he found along the upper streams or off the main trails were sufficient to keep his hopes alive. And, as he was fond of telling those who thought him a fool, just being in such peaceful surroundings was reward enough; striking it rich would be gravy.

After nearly an hour of making his way up the mountain, Bones reached a wide bend in the trail and came across a middle-aged man wading in a nearby stream, panning for gold in the same manner Callahan had demonstrated to the tourists earlier. The other prospector glanced up from his work and nodded a greeting.

"Howdy," Bones said. "Any luck today?"

"Little dust, but that's it."

The two men had run into each other along this mountain stretch a couple of times the past week, and although they'd never bothered to introduce themselves to each other by name, they shared the easy friendship of longtime acquaintances. They were bound, no doubt, by the brotherhood of their mutual hobby.

"Where's that cute little thing with the camera?" the man in the stream asked Bones as he waded to shore.

"She's my niece," Bones told him. "She's on her way, but I wanted to get in some time alone."

"You two making some kind of movie?"

"Yeah, something like that," Callahan said. "No big thing."

The other prospector climbed out of the water and lowered the brim of his cap to ward off the late-afternoon sun as he looked up at Bones. "You wouldn't happen to be usin' some bikers in that movie, would you?"

"No," Bones said. "Why do you ask?"

The other man scratched the back of his head. "Well, I've been hearing motorcycles puttering around up here the past couple days, and seein' how there's not much call for 'em bein' up here, I just fig-ured . . ."

"Well, they aren't with us, that's for sure," Bones said, holding his steed steady on the trail. "We did have a little run-in with 'em yesterday, though, mat-ter of fact."

"Yeah?"

"Yeah. My niece was filmin' me doin' some pan-ning when we saw these biker guys the next hill up, lookin' like they were doin' some serious dig-gin' . . . like they thought they were lookin' for pirate treasure instead of gold. We didn't pay 'em no mind, but they come down anyway and started askin' a lot of questions.''

''What kind of questions?''

''Just wondered if they were gonna end up in our movie, what kind of movie we were shootin'... stuff like that.''

''Nosy, just like me, huh?'' the other man said with a grin.

''Well, yeah,'' Bones said. ''Only I feel a lot more comfortable around you. Those guys gave me the creeps. I'm tellin' ya, a ranger pulled by on one of the fire breaks and I'm glad he did, 'cause I was half expectin' these bikers to try helpin' themselves to my niece's camera and all my gear.''

The other man shook his head in disgust. He was chewing a plug of tobacco, and he spat a brown stream of juice into the dirt next to him. ''Shit,'' he complained, ''I don't know about you, but I come up here to get away from that kind of riffraff. Damn shame when they gotta come up and spoil somethin' pretty as this.''

''Amen to that,'' Callahan agreed as he tugged on his horse's reins. ''Well, I think I'll be headin' upstream a bit. Y'all have a good one, hear?''

''You bet.''

Before Bones could resume his trek up the mountain trail, there was a sudden commotion in the brush just uphill from the stream. It was a thrashing sound, growing louder and closer by the second. Loose dirt and gravel began to pound down onto the trail around him, and as he glanced up the steep slope of the mountain, he realized with horror what was happening.

"Landslide!"

Bones tried to calm his animals, but between the thunder of the avalanche and the quaking of the ground, both were spooked and Callahan was thrown from the saddle when the horse reared. He landed hard on his right hip, swearing at the jolt of pain that shot down his leg. The other prospector rushed forward, reaching for the reins, but both the horse and mule ran off, the pounding of their hooves drowned out by the increasing roar of the slide. Bones straggled to his feet and the other man tried to help him to cover, but it was already too late. Larger stones and man-sized boulders had now joined the downhill tumble, and before they could get clear, the avalanche crashed down on them, sending both men sprawling like scattered tenpins. The man in the hip boots let out a cry that died in his throat as his head was crushed by a monstrous, tumbling slab of rock. He landed facedown in the soft earth near the stream, bleeding into the mud. The last wave of the slide swept over him, half burying him in a heap of loose stone and gravel. As the sickening boom of the slide echoed its way downhill and the ground fell still along the creek bed, it was clear that the fallen man was dead.

Bones had managed to survive the landslide, but both his legs had been broken by the impact of a rolling boulder. He lay in pain seven yards from the dead man, pinned against a pine tree by a mound of debris. Callahan knew that there was always a chance of a second slide, and that somehow he had to find a way to get to better cover. There was an escarpment to his right that would provide a buffer against any future slide, but it was more than thirty yards away, an insurmountable distance given his condition. He tried calling out to his mule and pack horse, but he suspected it was a futile gesture. Provided the animals had weathered the slide, they were likely far gone from this part of the mountain.

Behind him, Bones detected the crunch of gravel, and his spirits rose.

"Stubborn?" he called out again, twisting his torso for a better look. Instead of his mule, however, Bones saw a man approaching him. He was in his late twenties and had his long hair tied back in a ponytail. He was wearing a black leather jacket and dusty jeans.

"You," Bones groaned, recognizing the man. "Help me..."

"Sure thing, pops." The man took note of the dead prospector, then bent over long enough to hoist a twenty pound rock from the pile of debris pinning Bones against the pine tree. Grinning at the look of horror in Callahan's eyes, the man heaved the rock directly at his head. "Here, catch!"

Bones threw up one arm and partially deflected the rock, but it still came crashing into his face with so much force that he was knocked unconscious. The man stepped closer and crouched next to Callahan, checking his wrist for a pulse. Finding one, he picked up the same boulder he'd thrown before. This time, standing directly over Callahan, the man raised the rock high above his head, drawing aim again on Bones's skull.

"Poor bastard," he sniggered, heaving the rock down with all his might. "This just isn't your day...."

PAMELA CALLAHAN was running late, as usual.

It seemed to her that Denver was becoming more and more like Los Angeles every year. The roadways were becoming increasingly choked with vehicles whose drivers were either in a big hurry to get into the city or to leave the capitol behind and reach the comforting confines of their ever-growing suburban neighborhoods. What years ago had been a quick jaunt down to Colorado Springs was now a major expedition, and by the time Pamela turned off Interstate 25 and headed west toward Rayford's Creek, the sun was already on the verge of falling behind the lofty summit of Pikes Peak.

"He's going to have a fit," she muttered under her breath as she shifted into overdrive and stepped on the accelerator to force her '86 Mustang up the steep rise of the main access road. She'd promised her Uncle Bones she'd be by shortly after four so they could beat the dinner rush at the Wild Creek Inn. She knew how much he hated crowds, and she wanted him to be as much at ease as possible when she gave him the good news—that she'd gotten the funding to finish her documentary film in time to qualify for next week's Manitou Springs Film Festival. Rising to a challenge posed by her uncle, she'd snuck into a board meeting of Tallmount Mining Incorporated and had replaced an instructional video with footage from her uncompleted film. The board had been incensed at first, but after they'd viewed the work she'd done, members passed a motion to underwrite the project's completion. It had been quite a coup, requiring the kind of spunk and determination Bones Callahan was known for, and Pamela looked forward to seeing the expression on his face when she told him the story.

There were two access roads to Rayford's Creek, one a wide thoroughfare that beelined to its destination from the freeway but was choked with traffic. Pamela opted for the second route, a winding, two-way road that snaked through the mountains. It was a more indirect way to the Gold Rush Daze site, but there was far less traffic and Pamela thought she could pick up some time. For the first mile, in fact, she had the southbound lane to herself and she inched a few miles past the speed limit, taking corners with skillful ease. Her window was down and the wind blew freely through her long blond hair. Radio reception was sporadic, so she popped in a cassette and sang along to the latest album by Los Lobos, an L.A. band whose East L.A. roots came through loud and clear in every song. The lyrics reminded her of her youth back in Southern California, when she lived adjacent to the barrio and had spent many a good time with her Hispanic neighbors.

She was recalling childhood evenings playing hide-and-seek with the Blancanales family when she suddenly noticed a car in the rearview mirror, picking up speed as it closed in on her. She reflexively eased her

foot off the accelerator, wary that it might be an unmarked police cruiser. As she turned down the vol-
ume on her tape player, Pamela kept an eye on the
mirror. As the other car drew closer, she could see it
was a dust-covered Buick with a crumpled front fen-
der, hardly the sort of pursuit vehicle the law would
have at its disposal.

Up ahead was a sharp bend in the road, and there
was a precipitous drop-off just beyond the guardrail
flanking the opposite lane. Pamela lightly touched the
brakes to slow down, figuring the Buick would do the
same. Instead, the other car lunged forward at the last
second, slamming into her rear bumper just as she was
negotiating the turn.

''What the—''

Fighting the steering wheel, Pamela tried to keep her
car under control as she felt herself swerving across the
dividing line. Fortunately there was no traffic coming
in the opposite direction, because before she was able
to avoid going into a full tailspin, Pamela had crossed
the other lane and glanced against the guardrail,
denting the side of her car but managing to keep it
from plunging down the cliff.

The Buick, meanwhile, was coming up on her right
and veering sharply to its left, pushing her car back
into the guardrail again. It took all her reflexes to retain a semblance of control over the vehicle, and it was
only by flooring the accelerator and aiming straight
down the road that she was able to get free of her
pursuer. But even then the Buick continued to race
closely behind her.

Just ahead, a trio of cars were heading Pamela's way. Hoping to draw their attention to her plight, Pamela began swerving from side to side and holding her hand down on the car's horn. Finally, when she'd gained a good twenty yards on the Buick, she hit the brakes and sideswerved to a stop, blocking both lanes of traffic. The oncoming cars had no choice but to slow to a stop.

The Buick, however, slowed down just enough to pull onto the dirt shoulder nearest the mountainside, then reverse its course and speed off in the opposite direction. Pamela alertly glanced at the retreating vehicle and took note of its license number, then scribbled it on a scrap of paper beside her. As the Buick disappeared around the bend, Pamela exhaled and finally realized how much she was shaking.

The driver in the front car that she'd blocked got out and came over to her stalled vehicle. He was an elderly man with bifocals and was wearing an oversized suit.

"What's the problem here, miss?"

Pamela quickly explained what had happened and jotted down the license number again on another piece of paper. Handing it to the man, she said, "In case you get to a phone before I can, would you call the police and have them look out for this car? I was nearly killed."

He looked at the fresh dents in the rear of Pamela's car and then at the slip of paper. "Do what I can, miss. You need any help?"

She shook her head. "No. I don't think there was any major damage done, so I'm going on ahead to Rayford's Creek. I'll call the police from there."

"You're sure you're all right?"

Pamela nodded and restarted the engine. She drove around the man, who had headed back to his car, and offered an apologetic look to the people in the other vehicles she'd blocked. One driver shouted something at her, but she didn't pay attention to the insult. Her mind was still racing, trying to make sense of what had just happened. She realized that in all the commotion she hadn't had a good chance to look at whoever was driving the Buick. Who could have wanted to do something like that to her? She didn't think she had any enemies, at least none that would resort to such drastic measures.

Slowly her pulse returned to normal, and the rest of the ride passed without further incident. Gold Rush Daze was closing for the day when she pulled off the Rayford's Creek exit, and she could see children in the back seats of departing vehicles chewing Gold Nugget gum and waving their souvenir picks and shovels and inflatable mules. Trying to take her mind off her ordeal, Pamela recalled her own childhood in L.A. and the times when Uncle Bones would drop by to take her and her brother Nick out on some memory-filled outing to a local tourist haunt, any outing that would contrast sharply with the tension-filled atmosphere at home, where her mother was slowly deteriorating from multiple sclerosis and her father was seldom home because he needed to work three jobs to make ends meet. What a savior he'd been back then. Now, with her parents both gone and Nick working overseas in Great Britain, he was the only family she had left.

After pulling into the Gold Rush Daze parking lot, she got out of her car and headed for a phone booth, determined to call the police. She heard the humming of rotors and glanced toward the hills, where a small Bell helicopter was floating down toward the creek with some sort of cargo dangling beneath it. She only gave the sight passing notice, then went to the phone and put in a quarter. Before she could dial, however, Emily came up beside her and placed a hand on her shoulder.

"Pamela..."

The moment she looked at the other woman, Pamela felt a cold shudder of dread, and without a word being spoken she knew that something was terribly wrong. All the while, the helicopter was drawing nearer, heading for the parking lot, where a lone paramedic van was just pulling up behind Pamela's Mustang. Pamela's gaze was drawn back to the chopper and the objects suspended beneath it. There were two bodies, both of them already enclosed in thick black bags.

"No!" she gasped, leaning into Emily's protective embrace as she continued to gaze at the bodies. Two attendants came out of the paramedic van and brought over a gurney, setting it down on the ground and then crouching low so the Bell could come lower and carefully set the wrapped corpses on top of it. Once the bodies were freed from the supporting cables, the chopper rose and drifted away. The attendants rolled the gurneys back to their van.

"Uncle Bones!"

Pamela sobbed and ran forward, bidding the attendants to pause before loading the bodies. Gesturing for them to unzip one of the bags, she drew in a deep breath, summoning all her courage. When she looked down and saw her uncle's bruised and lifeless face, she felt a sudden pang of emptiness engulfing her.

And then Bones Callahan was gone.

Pamela watched the van pull away from the lot and head toward the main access route back to Colorado Springs. Emily remained close beside her, and finally she said, "I'm so sorry, Pamela. He was such a good man. I just can't believe such a freak accident could have—"

"It was no accident," Pamela said with cold conviction, wiping a single tear from her cheek. "My uncle was murdered...."

1

Like some hungry monolithic beast, the five-ton power shovel bit into the hard Virginia soil and came up with its powerful metallic jaws full of dirt, then hauled the load to a waiting dump truck already half-filled with a day's worth of digging. As the shovel swung back to the hole for yet another scoop, two men watched approvingly.

"Should have the pool in there by August, right?" Carl Lyons speculated.

"Labor Day is what Bear told me," Gadgets Schwarz countered, "but my money says it's gonna be just like any other construction project, which means more likely Thanksgiving."

"Yeah, maybe so, but I'll take it whenever I can get it, no complaints."

"Amen to that," Schwarz said. "After all these years of working out in those cramped barracks, this is gonna be heaven."

The two men were speaking about a fully equipped gymnasium that was about to be erected on the grounds of Stony Man Farm, a remote patch of private land surrounded by the Blue Ridge Mountains in the heart of Shenandoah National Park. The true purpose of the retreat was in no way indicated by its surface appearance, and any vacationer taking a hot-air balloon tour over the area might easily have mistaken the compound for the estate of some retired Virginia gentleman. In reality, Stony Man Farm was far from being the lair of some middle-aged aristocrat, and the two men overlooking the work on the gymnasium were hardly muscle-bound workhands assigned to their latest construction project.

Along with colleague Pol Blancanales, the trio collectively known as Able Team were the veterans of untold skirmishes with the more deadly and undesirable elements that had inflicted their misery on the globe in recent years. Be they international terrorists, KGB operatives, psychopaths, drug smugglers, mafia wise guys or callous opportunists with no regard for human life—at one time or another Lyons, Schwarz and Blancanales had gone up against them and emerged victorious—at least to a degree. The nature of evil in the modern world was such that stomping out one foe was no guarantee that two or three equally loathsome opponents wouldn't crop up in their place. It was the sad nature of the game, a fact that each of the men knew but tried not to dwell on. It was better to hope that one day their efforts might do more than briefly stem the tide. Better to hope that if they kicked enough low-life ass, they'd eventually put themselves out of a job because the world was finally at peace with itself. A foolish notion, perhaps, but it helped.

The Team had earned its scars and stripes, and although none of them was getting any younger, the rigors of their profession had kept their bodies in prime physical condition. When completed, the gymnasium would provide the men with a chance to maintain such conditioning in a controlled environment away from the field of battle. They'd won the right for such facilities several months back when, on behalf of Hal Brognola, their commander and White House liaison, they'd tested the newest presidential security arrangements and had slipped past the Secret Service to make a simulated hit on the Chief Executive. Having lost their bet that the Service could ward off any and all possible assailants, the Feds had ruefully appropriated the necessary funds for the fitness center. Most of the main building was well on the way to completion, but the pool annex was just past the ground-breaking stage.

"Well, they aren't going to get this sucker finished today," Lyons told Schwarz, "so we might as well get back and see about this new assignment Hal's got cooking. You got any clue what it's gonna be?"

Schwarz shook his head as they fell into long strides. "I overheard something about Washington, but with Pol heading to Colorado for that funeral, I'd guess we'll probably end up plugged into the Rockies somewhere. You know the chief...."

"Yeah, you're probably right," Lyons reflected. "At least it's nice out there this time of year."

"You make it sound like we'll be going out there for some R & R."

"Wouldn't mind that one bit."

"Wouldn't count on it, either."

The main house was only forty yards away. The midday sun poured down on its back porch, where the team's crack flyboy, Jack Grimaldi, was engrossed in a game of chess with weaponsmith John Kissinger.

"Hey, guys," Grimaldi yelled when he noticed their approach. "Hope your hiking boots are in good shape."

Schwarz cast Lyons a sidelong glance and grinned. "What'd I tell you?"

In unison, Kissinger and Grimaldi dipped into the John Denver songbook and began serenading, "Rocky Mountain high, Colorado..."

"We're going along with Pol, eh?" Schwarz said.

Grimaldi nodded as he maneuvered his last remaining knight around Kissinger's bishop. "Check."

Kissinger frowned a moment, then nonchalantly brought his queen into play, sweeping it halfway across the board to capture Grimaldi's knight. Affecting an Australian accent, he countered, "Check, mate."

Lyons used the necessary code to open the steel access door leading into the house. Schwarz followed him down a set of steps to the basement, where Hal Brognola was waiting for them in the War Room. The mastermind behind Stony Man's global operations, Brognola had the look of someone unfamiliar with the notion of a full night's sleep. There was a telltale wash of fatigue in his eyes and a tiredness in his deep, sonorous voice.

"Hello, boys," he told them. "Pull up and take a load off."

The men obliged him, sitting around the government-issue table, where they'd gathered more times than they cared to remember. Theirs was a grueling sort of war, one fought without any public recognition and without any official sanction. One could search through the billions of government documents choking the nation's capitol a mere sixty miles away and never come across mention of Stony Man Farm or Able Team or any of it participants, for the nature of their ongoing mission precluded any link to an aboveground organization. Why? For the simple reason that when Able Team went up against a foe, the men didn't take the rule book with them and they neither expected nor offered any quarter from the enemy. Congress and the ACLU had no leash on them, and so long as they did their job effectively and as clandestinely as possible, they were able to avoid the accountability measures that made so many contemporary law enforcement groups feel hamstrung.

"Jack says we're going to Colorado," Lyons told Brognola to start things off. "I assume it's not because the Nuggets made the playoffs this year."

"You assume right." Brognola pulled three manila files from a briefcase next to him and passed them around.

"Something about this friend of Pol's who died?"

Brognola nodded. "Personal favor to Pol. He's up packing now. You can join him."

"What's the bottom line?" Lyons wanted to know. "All we know is that some guy Pol grew up with was crushed in an avalanche. Hardly up our line. They need guys with good backs to be pallbearers?"

"No jokes on this one, Ironman, okay?" Brognola said tiredly. "Pol's real shook up about it and I don't think he'd appreciate the wisecracks."

"Fair enough," Lyons said, "but I still don't see why this should concern us."

"Well," Brognola explained, "the guy's niece has it in her head that her uncle was murdered and that someone's out to get her, too. She doesn't know who, but there seems to be enough circumstantial evidence to back her up. There are some people looking into it out there, but Pol wants to make sure the investigation doesn't get swept under the carpet."

"And . . ." Schwarz said.

"What do you mean?" Brognola said.

"I mean, nice guy that you are, you still wouldn't give us the green light to head out to Colorado just to do a little gumshoe work. It's not our turf. Let's get to the 'as long as you're out there' part."

Brognola chomped on his ever-present cigar and then smiled thinly at the other two men. "Am I really that predictable?"

"Aye, aye, sir," Lyons said.

"Well, so be it." Brognola sighed and skimmed over a file in front of him on the desk. "I checked in at NSC to see if there was anything out in Colorado up your alley. Turns out there's some cloak-and-dagger going on in Air Force Intelligence."

"What else is new," Lyons said.

Brognola went on, "Apparently a few weeks ago AFI was wrapping up a five-week investigation and ready to bust some corporal for selling secrets to a KGB intermediary when there was some kind of tip-off. A sniper scoped the rendezvous point. The corporal got a bullet in the brain and our guy nearly took one himself. The only real info that came out of the whole thing was that the Soviets were lining up some major connections around Colorado Springs in order to establish some kind of operating base in the mountains."

The chief passed along a one-page brief on the operation and Lyons and Schwarz huddled together to skim through it.

"From the sounds of it, despite that screwup they're still on top of things, so why not just let them keep running with it?"

"Two reasons," Brognola countered. "First off, AFI suspects there might be some inside link to the KGB on this one and they don't want to go around setting off any more alarms than necessary. Secondly, and maybe more importantly, we have reason to believe that one of our old nemeses might be the new link to KGB operations in the Rockies."

Schwarz's eyes widened and he let out an expectant gasp. "Levdroko?"

Brognola nodded. "Oleg Levdroko. The one and only."

"Levdroko," Lyons muttered. "I'll be damned. I've always wondered if we'd get another shot at him."

"Well, that settles it," Schwarz said, pushing away from the table. "Come on, Ironman. We got ourselves a score to settle."

The two men left Brognola and bounded up two stories to the upper floor of the headquarters, where they found Pol Blancanales adding a few last items to a suitcase laid out on the bed. He nodded a greeting at both men and asked them, "Coming along, then?"

"You got it, Pol," Lyons said. "Sorry again about this friend of yours. Tough break."

"Yeah," Blancanales said, sitting down on the edge of the bed as he put his shoes on. "It's hard to explain, but next to my old man, Bones Callahan was the closest thing I had to a father figure when I was living in East L.A. A great guy. Had season tickets to Dodger Stadium and must have taken me at least a dozen times a year. Helped steer me away from the gangs, too."

"You keep in touch with him?"

"Sort of," Pol said. "Not nearly enough, though. You know how it goes."

"Yeah," Schwarz said.

"I just can't believe he's gone," Pol said. "Doesn't seem right."

"What's this about his niece?"

"I'm not sure," Pol confessed. "Last time I saw her, she was just nineteen, fresh out of high school. She ran around with my kid sisters, so we weren't really all that close. If she thinks there's foul play, though, I'll take her word for it." He closed the lid on his suitcase, a little more forcefully than necessary. "And if she's right, I pity the poor bastard behind it. They'll pay, damn it. They'll pay...."

2

The corporate headquarters for Denver Technological Incorporated, ironically, wasn't located in Denver at all, but rather twenty-one miles southeast of the capitol in Parker, a small, relatively slow-paced town. Parker was noted primarily for its claims to be the only city in Colorado operating in the black. Prior to incorporating earlier in the decade, Parker had been something of a one-horse town with a sparse, scattered population. In recent years, however, the number of building permits had increased substantially and the burg was slowly transforming itself into a bedroom community filled with its share of commuters who spent their days in Denver. Denver Tech had made a sizable contribution to the march of progress, becoming the primary tenant of the renovated Old Road Carriage House, which anchored the newly erected Parker Mall on Main Street.

As he parked his green Cadillac in front of his firm's offices, retired Air Force General Buck Howser waved to the gangly sixteen-year-old sweeping the front walk.

"Mornin', General," the youth called out as he waved back at the tall, strapping man who'd just gotten out of the Cadillac. Although Howser could still wear the same size uniform he wore when he entered the service during the Korean War, today he had on a somber gray suit with barely visible pinstripes. The only tip-off of his former profession was the gold-plated B-1 clasp holding his tie in place.

"Good Morning, Floyd." Howser bent over and snatched up an empty soda can from the parking lot and tossed it to the youth. "How's the hook shot today?"

Floyd caught the can with his left hand and stopped sweeping long enough to make a surprisingly graceful move to his left, imitating Kareem Abdul-Jabbar's famed sky hook. The can arched high, just missing the overhang covering the sidewalk, then clattered into a trash bin. Floyd beamed as he turned back to Howser. "Three-point play."

The General gave the youth an encouraging smile as he headed for the main entrance. "Keep it up and you'll make all-county this winter."

"I sure hope so."

Entering the Carriage House, Howser traded pleasantries with a few of the employees who ran the downstairs shops, including Myke Brooks, the cherub-faced woman behind the counter of the newsstand.

"Running late for your board meeting," she told him as she handed over the morning edition of the *Denver Times*. "They were just down here asking about you."

"Got tied up on the way over," Howser said.

"Nothing serious, I hope."

Howser shook his head but his easygoing smile stiffened as he tucked the paper under his arm and started up the oak staircase leading to the second floor. He nodded a terse greeting to the receptionist stationed in the front room of the Denver Tech suite, then passed through a pair of double doors and into a long corridor filled with various turn-of-the-century artifacts that tied in with the look of the restored building. Halfway down the hall, he turned into a side room, entering a conference chamber where four other members of the corporation's board of directors were already seated around an antique tiger-oak desk.

"Sorry, folks," he told them as he moved around to one of the two vacant chairs and sat down. He sighed and all pretense of good cheer left his tanned, weathered face.

Herm Salas, seated to Howser's left, drummed his pudgy fingers along the edge of his coffee cup as he said, "Chuck's not with you?"

"No," Howser said, shooting a quick glance at the still-empty chair. "I don't think he's going to be showing up, either."

"Why not?"

Howser had brought an attaché case with him, and as he unsnapped the clasp and opened it, he took in the other board members with a dismal glance. "Unless I miss my guess," he said, "Chuck Cosvie's probably out of the country by now."

"What?" Salas exclaimed. Several of the other board members likewise gasped with surprise.

"You can't be serious," Richard Natore said.

"I wish I wasn't, believe me," Howser said, taking out a manila file and passing it to his fellow board member. "But I just got back from a meeting with Clyde Wheat from accounting and Frank Loworth at the district attorney's office up in Denver."

"The D.A.?" Salas said. "What's going on here?"

"As near as we can figure at this point," Howser explained, summarizing the information in the file Natore was glancing through, "Cosvie embezzled nearly four million dollars out of our till and made himself scarce over the weekend."

"Chuck? An embezzler?" Salas scoffed at the notion. "That's the most ridiculous thing I've ever heard. Why, I'd trust him with my life. He and I go back, way back."

"Well, you better take a good look at that file before you rush to defend him," Howser advised the board's senior member. "I felt the same way about his integrity, despite all our differences, but this info puts it in an all new light."

"Incredible," Natore muttered, shaking his head as he closed the file and handed it over to Salas and the other board members.

For the better part of forty-five minutes, the scheduled meeting was put on hold while the members came to terms with the grim facts Howser had brought to their attention. All in all, it was a bleak revelation. Cosvie, who had founded DTI along with Buck Howser and Herm Salas in the late seventies, had apparently used his computer expertise to juggle the company books in recent months. He had siphoned off large chunks of capital into a self-owned shadow company operating out of a post office box in neighboring Aurora. That company, Boulevard Enterprises, had soaked up 3.9 million dollars in DTI funds, only to turn up with empty coffers when Clyde Wheat had finally stumbled onto Cosvie's machinations and gone to the authorities. A search of Cosvie's vacated condominium had turned up clues pointing to a standby flight to South America and possible money transfers to the Cayman Islands. There weren't enough specifics at this stage to give hope that either Cosvie or the missing funds would be found quickly, if ever. Howser had already been in touch with company lawyers, who said that some of the loss would be covered by insurance.

"The bottom line, though," Howser continued, "is that our cash flow situation is shot to hell, and Cosvie couldn't have picked a worse time to pull this off in terms of our vulnerability."

"Hey, tell us something we don't already know," Natore grumbled, still shaking his head at the news. "Losing that SDI contract was already one nail in our coffin. This could really put us in the grave."

Natore was referring to a long- and hard-sought defense contract that would have bailed DTI out of its recent financial slump by bringing in thirty-seven million dollars in new business. It would have given the company responsibility for the development of computer applications for those few space-age weapons systems that were to survive the massive cutbacks to the Star Wars program. The contract was considered a must for DTI, which had fallen on lean times the past three years due to stiff competition both at home and abroad. To lose that bid and then discover that one of their own founders had picked the company clean was almost more than the board members could deal with.

"So where does that leave us?" Salas muttered. "Do we have to go Chapter Eleven? Bankruptcy court? Shit, I thought I'd never see the day..."

"There is one alternative," Howser suggested.

"What?" Salas groaned. "Hire Charles Bronson to go track Cosvie down and bring our money back?"

Howser shook his head and sorted through his attaché case for another file. "We could consider the Mountland merger...."

"Not that again," Salas spat contemptuously.

"No, wait," Natore interrupted. "Buck might be onto something here."

"Bullshit," Salas said. "We voted that motion down seven months ago. It's as good as dead in my book."

"A lot's happened in those seven months," Natore reminded Salas and the others. "Let's at least take another look at it."

"Can we make that official new business?" Howser seconded, looking out at the others. His motion was quickly passed and another lengthy discussion ensued, deliberating the pros and cons of merging with Mountland Computer Enterprises. Cosvie and Salas had previously opposed the deal and the motion had gone down to defeat when the vote split the board down the middle. Today, however, despite Salas's continued opposition, the motion passed, three votes to two.

"Of course, our lawyers will still have to iron things out and make sure Mountland's receptive to the idea," Howser said once the decision had been made. "But I think we've acted in the best interests of the firm. We'll be better off on our feet in a partnership than on our backs alone."

"I still think it's a mistake," Salas groused. "I just hope we don't live to regret it."

"Just swallow your pride a moment and it'll all work out," Natore told the older man.

There were a few other items of unfinished business, none of them significant in light of what had already transpired at the meeting. They were dealt with quickly, then the meeting adjourned. Howser lingered behind, answering questions and exchanging a few more remarks about Cosvie's actions and the possible repercussions it might have on DTI's future. He did his best to put on an optimistic front, assuring everyone that the storm could be weathered, especially now that they'd committed themselves to the merger.

Finally the others left and Howser found himself alone in the conference chamber. He poured himself a cup of coffee and moved over to a phone in the corner of the room. Dialing a number, he waited patiently until his call was answered on the third ring by a pleasant-sounding woman.

"Mountland Computer Enterprises," she said, "Mr. Greason's office."

"Cindy, this is Buck Howser," he told her. "Put Bill on the phone for me, would you? You can tell him up front it's good news...."

HOWSER AND GREASON had agreed to meet an hour later at Esensten and Brown, a run-down watering hole on the outskirts of Parker with a reputation for making the best burgers in all of Jefferson County. Like Howser, Wild Bill Greason had first put on a uniform during the Korean War and had pulled a full pension's worth of duty for the Air Force before retiring to nearby Lakewood. He was currently applying his military expertise as a consultant for several defense contractors based in Colorado, including Mountland Computer. Two inches shorter and twenty pounds lighter than Howser, Greason nonetheless cut a commanding figure as he sauntered through the bar in his tan slacks and navy blazer. Spotting Howser in one of the back booths, the general waved a greeting and paused long enough to place an order with the nearest cocktail waitress.

"Hello, Buck," he said when he slid into the booth across from Howser and shook the other man's hand. "Good to hear things went well with the board. Any surprises?"

"Not really," Howser conceded. "Salas put up a squawk and managed to keep Paulsen in his corner, but that was to be expected."

"Pity about Cosvie," Greason murmured, running a finger around the rim of his beer stein. "I'm sure he would have liked to throw another monkey wrench into our little plan."

"True," Howser reflected. "But Cosvie's not going to be throwing much of anything anymore."

Greason drained his beer when he saw the waitress coming over with a fresh pitcher and a glass for Howser. He picked up the tab while Howser filled their glasses. Once the woman left, the two men raised their drinks for a toast.

"So much for phase one," Howser proposed. "Here's to the next step."

"Amen." They met their mugs with a slight thunk, then each took a short sip. Greason glanced around to make certain no one was within earshot, then leaned forward in his seat and lowered his voice to a whisper. "So Cosvie's taken care of once and for all?"

"Yep."

"And that couple your boy thought might have seen something?"

"Guy's name was Bones Callahan," Howser confided. "He's already been taken care of. It was a niece he was with, gal by the name of Pamela. She should be out of the picture by now, too."

"Good, good," Greason murmured. "And I take it you had the body moved."

Howser nodded. "Randall dug him up and moved him to the compound. Nobody's going to find him there."

"Especially if they're looking for him in Venezuela." Greason chuckled. "That whole cover story was a stroke of genius, Buck, I gotta admit."

"Just following the first commandment, that's all," Howser reflected modestly. "Thou shalt cover thy ass from all angles whenever possible."

"Ah, rules to live by."

They both fell silent a moment, taking long draws from their beer steins. Then Greason pulled out a yellow legal pad and clicked his pen, telling Howser, "All right, let's get down to business. I figure this is the best way to set up the merger without drawing suspicion...."

The two men had been over the plan countless times over the past seven months, ever since Chuck Cosvie's vote had thwarted the first attempt at the merger. There were numerous details to tend to, and they wanted to make sure that each move was carefully orchestrated and executed so as to allow the master plan to evolve with a slow but safe certainty. The strategy had paid off thus far, ridding them of Cosvie under circumstances that would divert attention from the real reason for his sudden disappearance. Once the Callahan girl was disposed of, that whole chapter would be behind them and they could focus their full attention on the merger and all the gains it would bring to each of them.

They had been discussing their plan for less than fifteen minutes when Howser heard a telltale roar in the driveway outside the bar. Through a grease-stained side window he saw a ponytailed figure in a leather jacket guide his chopped Harley into a narrow parking spot between a Dumpster and Howser's Cadillac. The rider swung out of his seat and paused long enough to light a cigarette before heading for the side entrance. Entering the bar, he ran his fingers through his long brown hair as he scanned the main room. Seeing Howser and Greason, he signaled with his index finger that he'd be with them in a minute. He finished his cigarette at the bar, waiting for a double shot of Wild Turkey from the bartender. Then, drink in hand, he joined the two generals, sitting next to Howser, who shared the bikers gray eyes and chiseled features.

"So, Randall," Greason said casually, "your old man says your first day on the extermination job went okay."

"Mostly, yeah," Randall said. He had yet to look his father in the eyes, a fact that wasn't lost on Howser.

"Meaning what?" the elder Howser asked. "You have a problem with that broad again?"

"Nothing I can't handle," Randall insisted. "I got her apartment cased out, but she hasn't come back there since yesterday."

"Well, then start looking elsewhere," Howser snapped irritably. "Her job, her friends...you know what to do."

"Only so many of us," Randall reminded his father. "We can't be everywhere at once."

"If you had done the job right the first time, you wouldn't be having these problems."

"Look, don't start on me, okay?" Randall glared at his father and quickly belted down his bourbon. "It was a fluke she got away the first time. It's not gonna happen again."

"Yeah, and maybe it won't because she's tucked herself away in police custody somewhere," Howser snarled. As his anger rose, veins began to protrude along his neck and around his temples. His voice rose beyond a whisper, too, and Greason had to motion for him to quiet down before they drew attention from the other patrons.

"Easy, Buck," Greason said, playing peacemaker between father and son. "Let's not bust a gasket over this."

"I hate incompetence," Howser hissed, his gaze boring into his son.

"Off my case...General!" Randall retorted in a mocking voice. "I said I'd take care of her and I meant it, so do like the man says and chill out, okay?"

"You look like something that just crawled out of the gutter," Howser seethed under his breath. "You talk like something out of the gutter."

"Excuse me, but I've heard this one before and I know it by heart." Randall set aside his empty glass and stood up. He eyed Greason instead of his father. "That woman's history by this time tomorrow. You got my word."

"I've got a few connections with the law enforcement around here," Wild Bill told the younger man. "I'll see what I can come up with on her, see if I can't help smoke her out into the open for you."

"I'd appreciate it," Randall said. "You know where to reach me...."

Without acknowledging his father, Randall left the bar. Howser watched him get back on his bike and kick-start it to life, then pull out of the lot, just missing the Cadillac.

"Little shit takes after his mother, I'll give him that much," Howser muttered. "No respect."

"Cut him a little slack, why don't you," Greason suggested. "Ain't like it's his fault Don went down in Nam." He was referring to Howser's oldest son, one of the last American casualties in Indochina during the early seventies.

"Don't start into a lecture with me, Bill," Howser warned, "I'm not in the mood."

"Just a word to the wise, that's all," Greason said. "He already did a good job on Cosvie and this Bones guy, remember. Give him another crack at the niece and I bet he'll come through. Don't be so fucking rough on him."

"Rough? Shit, that's a laugh." Howser shook his head with disgust. "I let the guy freeload off me when he's nearly thirty and I even put him to work for me, just in hopes he'll quit hanging around them fucking biker gangs, and what kind of gratitude do I get? Soon as he's done doing his work, he's back out trying to get his colors."

"You're a real piece of work, Buck," Greason scoffed. "You got the kid working as a fucking hit man and you're worried 'cause he hangs out with a bad crowd? Wake up and smell the coffee, ace. Shit, he got some bikers to help him with Cosvie, so what's the problem?''

"I don't like bikers," Howser said emphatically. "He wants to wear a uniform, let him enlist and he'll find out what being a man is really all about."

3

Skyline Drive was the scenic way to traverse the length of Shenandoah National Park, and as she drove the winding strip of asphalt Lao Ti felt a warm tug of nostalgia at the sight of the regal Blue Ridge Mountains surrounding her on all sides. How many times had she hiked these mountains, even jogged their majestic heights in an effort to keep herself in prime physical condition? The peaks of Hawksbill Mountain and Reddish Knob stood out in sharp relief against the horizon, like broad-shouldered sentinels standing a patient vigil over one of the more pristine stretches of countryside in the nation.

And then there was Stony Man Mountain, just up ahead, its contours rendering the profile of a somber, skyward-gazing man that invariably reminded her of Hal Brognola.

Well before reaching that elevated pinnacle, Lao Ti slowed her Subaru and exited Skyline Drive, starting down an inconspicuous two-lane road that snaked through a dense belt of hardwoods and conifers. A quarter of a mile in, the road seemingly ended near a small picnic area set in a two-acre clearing. But Lao Ti knew the site was set up merely as a diversion for any curiosity seekers who might have strayed onto the road. Bypassing the parking lot, the woman, who was of Mongolian and Vietnamese descent, switched onto a private dirt road. It was located behind a thick row of hedges, and she drove another few hundred yards until she was forced to stop before the gateway to Stony Man Farm.

There was only one guard stationed at the gate, but Lao Ti knew that another four men were positioned close at hand along the tall stone wall surrounding the Farm, and that a dozen other security agents were on call elsewhere on the grounds.

As the man calmly approached her vehicle, Lao Ti took off her sunglasses and shook her black hair free from the elastic band that had held it up during the drive from Washington. The woman projected a vibrant beauty and aura of self-assurance as she smiled at the guard.

"Sorry, ma'am," the man said, "but this is private property. I'm going to have to...Lao Ti? Is that you?"

"Hello, Mickey," she said cheerfully. "Long time, no see."

"Yes, ma'am, it sure has been." The guard glanced inside the car and saw that the woman was alone. "Didn't have any word you were coming by."

"I wanted it to be a surprise," she said. "I've got a few weeks off and decided at the last minute to fly out."

"Well, I'm sure the gang will be glad to see you," Mickey told her. "At least those that are here."

"Oh no," she groaned. "Don't tell me the Team's out on assignment."

"Afraid so. You missed 'em by only a couple hours, too."

"Well, that'll teach me."

"The chief will be glad to see you, though, I'm sure. Cowboy's here, too. And Bear, of course."

The guard retreated to the gateway and opened the way for Lao, who drove past with a wave and headed for the main buildings. Construction crews were still at work on the new gymnasium/swimming pool complex. She had heard about the project when she'd met up with the Team in California a few months ago, but this was the first she'd seen of it. In fact, this was the first time she'd been back to the Farm since resigning her position with the Team nearly two years ago. She still bore a few telltale scars from the incident that had led to her decision to change vocational gears. While trying to help a mob informant avoid execution prior to grand jury testimony, Lao Ti had been gunned down at close range in an ambush on the outskirts of Cincinnati. After pulling through surgery, she'd flown back to her home in the Far East to recuperate, then had become involved with the earthquake studies that had eventually taken her back to the States as part of an international team based in Pasadena.

Although no longer an official member of the Stony Man operation, Lao Ti was still a welcome and recognized figure at the Farm, and after parking near the main house, she was led inside by another of the security guards. Not surprisingly, she finally caught up with her former colleagues in the War Room, where she'd spent many an hour in the past being briefed about the latest hot spots around the world.

"Lao Ti!" Brognola called out at the sight of the woman. "What a surprise!"

"Hi, chief!" she replied. "Bear..."

Aaron Kurtzman smiled at her from his wheelchair. "To what do we owe this honor?"

"I missed you guys," she said, trading affectionate hugs with John Kissinger. "Isn't that enough?"

"Good enough for me," Kissinger told her, motioning to a chair. "Sit down, let us know what you've been up to since that whole quake thing...."

He was referring to one of Able Team's toughest assignments the previous year, when they'd been called on to battle the terrorist Yellow River Brigade. In conjunction with KGB spymaster Oleg Levdroko, the group had nearly succeeded in using nuclear devices to trigger the San Andreas Fault into rupturing and causing the worst earthquake in U.S. history as a means of compromising the country's West Coast defense operations. Lao Ti had become involved in that case because of her earthquake expertise and the fact that she had just come back into the country when the crisis had begun to unfold.

"After that," she told the others, "things pretty much settled down, in all respects. The faults have remained stable for the most part, and our studies are coming along well. Any luck and we'll be making some major breakthroughs soon on the forecasting front.''

"Sounds good," Kurtzman said. "If you need any help on the computer front, though, you know who to come to."

"I sure do," Lao Ti said. "And what's been happening here?"

"Same old shit," Kissinger said. "We had a little run-in with the mob in Vegas, then banged around Florida and Skyler's Island cleaning up some drug operations."

"Sounds like you've been keeping busy." Glancing at the paperwork spread out on the huge conference table, Lao Ti went on. "That's a diagram for a Silkworm, isn't it?"

Kissinger nodded, tapping his pencil against the missile blueprint. "We're doing a little homework for the CIA."

"Oh, really?"

"You remember reading about the Chinese selling silkworms in the Middle East?" Brognola asked her.

"Yes, I do," Lao Ti said.

"Well, it's beginning to look like that's only the tip of the iceberg," Brognola said. "The Company figures there's a whole black market springing up in the Third World, and there's all kinds of retooled U.S. weapons and copycat systems showing up. I don't have to tell you the prospects if it doesn't stop."

"More bloodshed there, more terrorist activity here," Lao Ti guessed, "and probably bigger odds that some maniac's going to end up with his finger on the trigger of a nuclear bomb.''

Brognola nodded gravely. ''That's about the size of it.''

Lao Ti shook her head sadly as she looked over the various diagrams representing weapons that were beginning to show up in the arsenals of struggling nations. From grenade launchers and simple automatics to fully integrated missile systems—a wide array of instruments of death were helping to escalate tensions around the globe and increase the flow of innocent blood on streets from Beirut to Bangkok.

Glancing around the room, Lao Ti felt an involuntary shudder of dread crawl along her spine. She told the others, ''I'd forgotten what a cheerful little place this is....''

4

Coming down out of the cloud cover, Able Team suddenly found themselves gaping at the jagged, majestic spine of the Rocky Mountains from inside their Beechcraft Bonanza. Dozens of peaks rose more than ten thousand feet into the bracing Colorado air, most of them still mottled with the remains of the previous winter's snowfall. The distant setting sun infused the terrain with a reddish-gold hue.

"How about we parachute down with skis on and race to the lodge?" Schwarz proposed.

"Yeah, right," Lyons said. "You and James Bond's stunt double can try that one all you want. I'll hold off on risking my neck until I really have to."

"Wimp," Schwarz taunted.

Lyons shot Gadgets a sardonic gaze. "Watch those four-letter words, or you'll be doing the high jump minus the chute."

"My, my, aren't we in a cheery mood."

"Hey, look," Lyons snapped. "Just give it a rest, okay?"

"Yeah," Blancanales piped in, trying to diffuse the confrontation. "Put your headphones on and watch the in-flight movie. It's one of your favorites."

There was, in fact, no movie, but Schwarz got the hint. He turned from Lyons and focused on an imaginary screen at the front of the cabin. "Oh, man," he cried out in mock excitement. "*Invaders of Uranus*. My favorite. Special effects like you wouldn't believe. I swear, there's this one scene when they've got the hemorrhoids flaring up and, damn, they look just like that thing in *Alien*."

Lyons tuned out Gadgets's banter and stared back out the window. Down below, melting snow on the flank of Mount Shavano had, as it did every spring, taken on the shape of a huge angel. Lyons vaguely remembered hearing the legend that the angel had first appeared last century when a Ute Indian chief had offered up a prayer on behalf of his friend George Beckwith, who at the time had been on his deathbed.

Death.

That's what was eating at Lyons, and he knew it. Sure, maybe it was Blancanales who was coming out here for a funeral, but Lyons had enough deaths on his mind to match Pol's grief and misery. For starters, although he was never much for sentiment, Lyons couldn't help but recall that it was the anniversary of his meeting Julie Harris. Julie had been a crack Bureau agent and as feisty an individual as one could ever hope to come across. They'd shared some good times, the two of them, finding reasons to smile and express tenderness in the midst of their ugly wars with world's undesirables. There had even been fleeting moments when he'd entertained the notion of marriage; a big step considering the sour taste his first go at the institution had left in his mouth. But he'd never had a chance to pursue the thought, much less propose, because Julie Harris had been gunned down by some lowlifes wreaking havoc inside one of the terminals at L.A. International. Lyons had taken the loss hard.

And then there was Tyne Murray, the femme fatale he'd gotten involved with during the Team's most recent mission. She was the first woman he'd gotten close to since Julie's death, and he'd fallen for her in a hard way, only to find out she was on the side of the enemy. She'd stood by and watched when Lyons had nearly had his chips cashed in, and when he'd cheated death yet another time, it had been his uncherished duty to fire the grenade blast that had sent Tyne to meet her maker. The irony had been almost too much for him. To have so misjudged a woman...he felt unclean at the mere thought of the whole sorry incident, as if it had been a deliberate desecration of the love he'd felt for Julia.

As the jet banked to the left and began its descent, Lyons gave one last look at the Angel of Shavano and whispered, "Happy Anniversary, Jewel...wherever you are."

"What's that?" Pol asked, glancing at Lyons.

"Nothing," Lyons said. "Just wishful thinking. You doing okay, Pol?"

"Yeah," Pol said, staring out the window. "Just been thinking about old times. Guess death does that to a guy."

"Ain't that the truth," Lyons said.

They both fell silent. Schwarz had shut up, as well, and for the next few minutes the only sound in the cabin was that of the air conditioning. Up in the front of the plane, Jack Grimaldi was at the controls, guiding the Beechcraft parallel to the east facing of the Continental Divide. He cased out the ground below and, nine minutes later, brought the small plane down on a seldom-used airstrip just outside of Salida, a small, remote town located near the banks of the Arkansas River and an hour's drive west of Rayford's Creek. After rolling to a stop, he finally killed the jet's engines and left the cockpit, joining his companions as they climbed down from the aircraft to the sun-baked tarmac.

"The chief wasn't kidding when he said he wanted us to keep a low profile," Jack told the others as he looked around at their surroundings. "This is the middle of nowhere."

"Fine with me," Lyons muttered as the four men retrieved their luggage from a storage compartment. "The fewer people around, the less politics we have to play."

Taking one of the Farm's planes had spared them the bother of having to explain why their bags were stockpiled with enough armaments to take over an entire airport. From their retooled Government Model Colts to a handful of M-16s and M-203 grenade launchers, the men had come prepared for a firestorm. It was something they would do their best to avoid but wouldn't duck from if it needed to be fought.

An old Dodge Royal Sportsman rolled across the airfield toward them. Behind the wheel was a middle-aged man with a receding hairline and dark pockets of flesh drooping beneath his tired eyes. He wore a drab suit that needed pressing. The man also needed a shave. "Hey, gents," he introduced himself. "Jim Allanson, Jefferson County Sheriff's Department. My boss says I'm at your disposal, so just let me know what you guys want and I'll try to oblige. I know I look like hell, but it's been a rough couple days."

"We've been there, Jim," Schwarz assured Allanson. "No need to apologize."

Handshakes were exchanged while Able Team transferred its bags to the van. Grimaldi agreed to stay behind and make arrangements for the jet while Able Team rode with Allanson.

"We were told you're giving protective custody to the Callahan girl," Lyons said to their driver when everyone was settled in the van.

"That's right," Allanson said. "That'll be our first stop if you want. She's just down the road from here."

"Yeah, let's do that," Lyons agreed.

"When's Bones's funeral?" Blancanales asked.

"Day after tomorrow." The officer went on to give the details behind the service.

"So," Schwarz said when Allanson was finished, "did the coroner decide it was an accident?"

"For the record, yes," Allanson confirmed. As he drove, he briefed the others on the latest developments surrounding the death of Bones Callahan. "We combed the slide site all day, but we didn't see anything that would point to foul play," he said. "Everything points to just a bad piece of luck for both men."

"But you said, 'for the record,'" Pol mentioned. "Does that mean you're still thinking murder?"

Allanson nodded. "Some things seem just a little too, well, coincidental."

"Seems that at the same time Bones and his buddy were getting crushed, the niece nearly got herself bumped off a mountain road by some killer Buick. She was able to get a license number, and it turns out the car was stolen, so we're figuring there's gotta be some kind of connection."

"Is that all you have to go on?" Schwarz wondered.

Allanson shook his head. "A couple hours after all this happened, somebody busted into Pamela's apartment up in Denver while she was still at the mortuary making funeral arrangements. Place was ransacked."

"For what?" Pol asked. "What were they looking for?"

"We aren't sure, exactly," Allanson confessed as he rounded a bend in the road. "Pamela says she has no idea who's behind this, and we're a little wary of taking her back to the apartment to see what might be missing."

"Why?"

Allanson shrugged. "We're not the big leagues and we'll be the first to admit it. It's not like we've got the resources to guarantee that she'd be safe from whoever might be lying in wait for her if we took her back. Know what I mean?"

Lyons nodded. "Yeah, we've played that game and come away with scars from it."

"How's she taking it?" Pol asked.

Allanson grinned ruefully. "Let's just say she's not thrilled with the idea of protective custody."

"I'M GOING BACK tomorrow, and that's final," Pamela told the bald man across from her. There was a harsh edge to her voice and the man put a finger to his lips in hopes of quieting her down. The other patrons in the dining room were glancing their way.

"Please, Ms Callahan. Not so loud."

"I should tell them all you're holding me hostage," she whispered curtly before biting into her spinach salad. "How would you like that?"

"We're doing our best to accommodate you, Ms Callahan," the bald man reminded her. "This arrangement beats having you cooped up in a safe house. Trust me."

"I don't want to talk about it."

They were at the Depot Hotel, a rustic inn near the river's edge that had formerly been a turn-of-the-century rail station used in the transport of ore from the mines upstate in Leadville. Built of brick and pine, the place had a nostalgic ambiance supplemented by the display of old mining gear, housewares and sepia-tone photographs of Salida during its early years. Bones Callahan had first taken his niece and nephew to the inn for Pamela's college graduation present, and she fondly recalled the tales he had spun to them that night by the huge stone hearth in the lobby. It was those memories that had prompted her to decide on the Depot when the men from the sheriff's department had told her it was imperative that she not return to her apartment in Denver for the next couple of days. This seemed a fitting place to mourn her uncle, and she was upset that the men couldn't grant her some space and some more time to herself.

A wave of grief swept over her and tears welled in her eyes. As she reached for a napkin to dab them away, Pamela saw Jim Allanson appear in the main doorway long enough to nod to the bald man sitting across from her.

"They're here," the man told Pamela, reaching into his wallet and pulling out a twenty dollar bill to cover the check. "Are you finished?"

Pamela had barely touched her salad, but she nodded and rose from the table, composing herself as she followed the agent from the dining room. Outside they walked across the parking lot to a row of small cabins adjacent to the main hotel. They were only a few years old but care had been taken to match the historical look and feel of the Depot. The Dodge was parked next to the end cabin and three men were hauling their bags from the van. She recognized one of them and her spirits rose immediately.

"Rosario!" she called out, breaking into a run across the parking lot.

Pol turned to greet the woman and was surprised at what he saw. Pamela had done a lot of growing since he'd last seen her, and despite her grief, she was beautiful, even more so than he remembered.

"Hello, Pam," he told her as she rushed into his arms. He felt awkward at the intensity of her embrace, but before he could pull himself away from her, he felt the dampness of her tears on his cheek and so Pol held on to her a moment longer, whispering, "I'm sorry about your uncle."

"It was terrible," she whispered. "I'm so glad you're here. I wasn't sure if you'd get my message."

"My family knows how to reach me in an emergency," Pol told her. "I came as soon as I heard. I brought a couple friends along with me, too."

Blancanales introduced her to Lyons and Schwarz as they headed into the cabin, followed by the two sheriff's officers. As was often the case, Able Team was presented as part of a generic federal task force, and Blancanales was deliberately vague as to the nature of his current profession. Pamela didn't press him on it.

"I'm just glad you're here," she repeated. "I've been going out of my mind. These men are holding me here against my will."

"They have good reason, Pam," Blancanales told her, demonstrating the reason why he'd been nicknamed Politician years ago by his cronies. He set down his suitcase on one of the three single beds in the room, which also contained a small alcove with kitchen facilities. It was a cramped fit for such a large gathering, and the bald man excused himself, leaving Allanson behind as the county's lone representative.

"When we think it's safe for you to go back to Denver, they'll go along with you," Allanson told Pamela, referring to the Team.

"No offense, but I really don't think I need bodyguards," Pamela said, her temper flaring again. "And I want to go back tomorrow. I have a film to finish."

"We'll see," Allanson responded.

"See nothing!" Pamela snapped. "Look, I've been as cooperative as I can, but this has gone far enough! This film means a lot to me and it meant a lot to my uncle, too. He wanted me to finish it. Don't you people have any consideration at all?"

Allanson opened his mouth to say something but thought better of it. Pamela turned and stormed out of the room, leaving the men behind. Allanson looked at Able Team. "Like I was saying..."

Blancanales headed for the door. "I'll be right back," he told the others.

As Pol left the cabin, Allanson turned to Schwarz and Lyons and sighed. "Unless he's had some training in psych he isn't going to get anywhere with her."

"He's had training," Schwarz assured the officer. "And he learned it in the field, where it counts."

ACROSS THE RIVER from the Depot Hotel, Randall Howser tapped out a line of cocaine on the upturned mirror of his modified Harley Sportster. Rolling a five dollar bill into a makeshift straw, he placed one end against his left nostril and the other against the thin ridge of white powder. Inhaling deeply through his nose, he vacuumed half the line up into his sinus cavity, then repeated the gesture with his other nostril. There was the inevitable twitch and shudder as the drug entered his system, followed by the trickling medicinal taste down the back of his throat. Nice stuff. Purer than the last batch. Real smooth.

In the fading twilight, Randall reached into the back pocket of his jeans for a silver flask filled with bourbon. He downed its contents, then smacked his lips in pleasure. It was always good to get a sweet buzz on before making a hit. Tease those nerves to a state of full attention and make the moment so vivid that he'd be able to give it his full concentration. It sure as hell had worked when he'd offed that corporal a week ago. Piece of cake. He'd also been high during the killings of Chuck Cosvie and Bones Callahan, and in ways those experiences had been even more heightened. There was a greater sense of power somehow when the murdering came at close quarters, when he could look his victims in the eyes and sense their fear. It would have been a bonus if he could have come up face-to-face against Pamela. But with all the protection she was getting now, it didn't seem likely that he'd be able to get close to her. He'd had his chance with the Buick and blown it. Now he just had to concern himself with getting the job done right and forget the thrills.

He was hidden in the brush near a seldom-used firebreak, straddling his chopper and wearing the same denim-and-leather outfit he'd worn when triggering the slide the day before. His dark, intense eyes were shielded behind the light tint of his sunglasses. The right lens was prescription, curved to bolster his long-distance vision. When he raised his hunting rifle and peered through the high-powered scope, he had a clear view of the hotel and its scattered outbuildings. Once night fell he'd have to rely on the infrared adapter, but he'd had his share of luck with that, too. All he had to do was wait for the woman to come out into the open, take aim and pull the trigger. Such an easy way to earn eight thousand dollars . . . and to get the old man off his back.

The old man. Recalling their meeting earlier, Randall's jaw clenched in rage. Shit, did he hate that bastard. Always putting him down, rubbing his nose in the fact that he'd never lived up to the promise of his brother. Don this, Don that... Why can't you be more like him? Yeah, well, if Donny boy's such hot shit, why's he dead, old man? Answer me that. He's down in a hole somewhere being eaten by worms and I'm still around. Think about it, Buck.

He was still mulling things over when he saw a figure emerging from one of the cabins, heading toward the river. Raising his rifle, Randall squinted through the scope and grinned contentedly, placing his finger on the trigger.

"Howdy, bitch," he muttered under his breath, feeling his groin harden against the smooth contour of his gas tank. "Just come a little closer and say bye-bye. . . ."

BLANCANALES SAW Pamela standing on a widow's walk overlooking the river, which ran high and loud along the banks, crashing off of half-submerged trees and thick pilings that supported the lookout. He approached cautiously, stopping a few yards down the railing from her. Neither of them said anything, but she didn't make any move to walk away from him, either. They both stared down into the flowing river, each aware of the other's presence.

"The closer you are to someone, the harder it is to lose them," Pol reflected finally. "Your uncle was really special."

"You don't have to patronize me," Pamela sniffed. "I'll be all right."

"I'm sure you will. And I'm not one to patronize," Blancanales said. "I figured you knew me better than that."

Pamela's resistance wavered slightly and for the first time she tore her gaze from the river and glanced Blancanales's way. "He was a wonderful man," she said. "He was like a father to me."

"I remember," Pol told her. "There was a time he was that way with me, too."

Pamela nodded, wiping at her tears. "I used to be jealous whenever he'd take you fishing or to a ball game. I had no reason to be, of course, but he was always so thoughtful and giving that it was easy to think no one else mattered."

"Yeah." They were silent a moment, before Pol asked, "He and I fell out of touch the past few years. My fault mostly. What had he been up to?"

Pamela quickly told him about Bones's part-time job and his prospecting jaunts up into the mountains, concluding, "I really don't think he ever planned on finding any real fortune up there, at least not in terms of gold."

"Knowing him, probably not," Pol asked. "What was that you were saying about a movie?"

"I was making a quasi documentary," Pamela explained. "Just trying to capture a bit of what it was like for the old-time prospectors during the first gold strikes. Uncle Bones was the star...probably the only person with enough patience to put up with all the waiting and double takes."

"You just making this film for fun?"

"No," Pamela quickly countered. "There's a film festival in Manitou Springs next week. I was going to enter it. I still want to. There are a few shots I'm going to have to miss, but I want to get it in...for my uncle's sake, as well as my own. You should see him on the screen. He looks so romantic, like some old-time hero."

"I'd like to see that film when it's finished," Pol said.

Pamela's mood shifted abruptly again and she moved away from the railing, gazing angrily back at the cabins. "Who knows when that'll happen? I have to get to my editing equipment if I'm going to—"

Pamela was interrupted by a muffled crack off in the brush across the river, followed by the impact of a bullet against the railing two inches from her right hand. The bullet splintered the wood. Dumbfounded, she stared down at the railing while Blancanales's battle-trained instincts apprised him of the situation in time to take action.

"Down!" he shouted, lunging forward and grabbing her by the shoulders.

Even as they were diving for cover behind a thick wooden bench, a second and third shot slammed into the walkway around them.

"What on—"

"Stay here!" Blancanales advised her as he reached into his coat and came out with his .45 automatic. He drew in a quick breath, then sprang from his crouch and artfully rolled across the deck to the next closest bench. When no further shots came his way, he bounded to his feet and scrambled clear of the walkway, all the while keeping his eyes on the other side of the river. Silhouetted against the evening sky was the form of someone hurtling up from out of the brush astride a motorcycle. Dropping to a two-handed crouch, Blancanales readied his aim, but it was too late. The gunman had already cleared the rise and disappeared from view, although the dull roar of his Harley gave away his position.

Blancanales quickly analyzed the situation and found it wanting. From where he was standing, the river was more than thirty yards wide and too turbulent to swim across. The nearest bridge was more than five hundred yards to the north, in the opposite direc-.ion the biker was taking.

"Damn!" Blancanales seethed, kicking at the dirt in front of him as he stood near the riverbank.

Behind him, Lyons and Schwarz were rushing into view, followed by Jim Allanson and the bald sheriff's officer. "What happened?" Schwarz wanted to know.

"Looks like Pamela's whereabouts aren't a secret anymore," Pol replied.

5

The lights of Denver sparkled into life as darkness crept across the city, for this was not some sleepy burg where the sidewalks were rolled up at sundown. If anything, the capitol's pace seemed to quicken with the bustle of post rush-hour traffic, the drone of ships on the South Platte River and the clatter of trains along various north-south routes cutting through the heart of town. One of the fastest growing cities in the country, Denver was the epitome of the overachiever. Near the train-yard warehouse district north of downtown, it was possible to look over one's shoulders and see brightly lit skyscrapers reaching upward like concrete arms intent on seizing the moon, which dangled overhead like a bright and tempting bauble.

Mountland Distribution, a subsidiary of Wild Bill Greason's Mountland Computer Enterprises, was located in the warehouse district, occupying nearly an entire city block with its complex of storage and shipping outlets, fleet of delivery trucks and seven-story office building. Greason rode alongside Buck Howser in the latter man's Cadillac as they passed through the security gates and entered the facility. They'd just spent the past two hours dining with another member of their old-boy network of retired Air Force generals, Tom Christie. Christie, on the board of directors for Ryco/Kent, a firm specializing in strip-salvaging and metal recycling, was already a cog in Howser's master plan and had provided assistance in earlier enterprises. With the pending DTI/Mountland merger, the stakes would be rising and increased participation from Ryco/Kent would be necessary to pull things off.

"I think we can count on him," Howser mused as he pulled into a parking spot near one of the larger warehouses.

"If he knows what's good for him, he'll come through," Greason amended.

"I think he knows," Howser said. "You saw the look on his face when we were talking about Cosvie. Tom knows damn well Cosvie isn't down in South America."

"Not unless they dug his grave real deep," Greason chortled.

Getting out of the Cadillac, the two men strolled leisurely up a flight of steps to the loading platform. Under the watchful eyes of two well-armed security guards, dock workers were transferring huge wooden crates into one of the semis backed up to the ramp.

"WH-32s," Greason said, pointing out one of the crates. "Made fifty-four of those bastards at eighty-five grand a pop before the bugs started turning up."

"I've always wondered what they looked like," Howser said.

"Well, there's no time like the present."

A forklift operator was wheeling out another of the crates when Greason motioned for him to stop. Grabbing a crowbar from a rack just inside the warehouse, the general carefully pried open the crate's lid, revealing a protective layer of contour-fitting foam rubber intended to protect the WH-32 during shipment. As Howser watched, Greason gently pulled off the foam sheath to expose the weapon, a sophisticated automatic grenade launcher that had been upgraded to handle more potent warheads. Although based on a design similar to the touted XM-174, the increased capacities had been realized at the expense of the reliability for which the older weapon was noted. Some of the flaws were negligible, such as shortened firing range and clumsiness of the tripod and pindle mounts, but the downfall of the WH-32 had been a major glitch in both the blow-back action and magazine mount. It was discovered that repeated firings seriously affected both parts, to the point where unexpected backfirings had killed eight soldiers in four different incidents taking place over a period of less than three weeks. An inquiry had quickly pinpointed the cause for the accidents and all production of the WH-32s had been brought to a halt. Half of the manufactured weapons had yet to be shipped and Mountland was stuck with them. The company had recently decided that it would be too costly and uncertain to retool the launchers to compensate for the design flaws, and had been forced to write off more than two million dollars in orders. It hoped to salvage five percent of its investment by selling off the weapons for scrap.

Or at least that was the official explanation.

"Nice-looking weapon," Howser said as he ran his finger along the oblong framework of the launcher. "Too bad it doesn't work."

"Well, once they strip it down at Ryco/Kent, it'll be reincarnated as parts for half a dozen other weapons," Greason said for the benefit of the forklift operator. "So it's not a complete loss."

In actual fact, both Greason and Howser knew that another fate was in store for the WH-32. Instead of being sent to Ryco/Kent, the launcher and its thirty other counterparts would be shipped to a nondescript warehouse near Saint Louis, where they would be repackaged and relabeled before being shipped overseas. the Saint Louis connection was run, not by another of the generals' fellow compatriots, but by U.S.-based KGB agents. The agents were part of the same network that ran the international shipping firm that would distribute the WH-32s to unsuspecting Iraquis and Koreans who thought they were paying top dollar for a welcome addition to their haphazard arsenals.

And the WH-32 scam was only the tip of the iceberg in terms of the growing empire overseen by Howser and his consortium of retired generals. From coast to coast, there was a network of individuals working in the shadows to milk the shortcomings of America's defense system. The procurement scandals that had rocked the Pentagon the previous year had curtailed some from carrying out private agendas, but Howser's cadre, with their inside contacts, had been able to stay one step ahead of investigators and take any needed measures to protect their cover.

"Okay, I've seen enough," Howser said, stepping back from the crate. Greason put the padding back in place, then carefully secured the lid before motioning the dockworkers to resume loading. The two men watched for a moment longer, then moved inside the building, where the night shift was tending to Mountland's vast inventory.

"Once we plug in DTI we'll be able to do some phasing out," Greason explained as he and Howser returned to their discussion of new strategies. "Knock out your deadwood, too, and we'll be in great shape for the new phase."

"That's what it's all about," Howser said. "I have a feeling this merger's going to be more than Salas can handle. We'll offer him a buy-out and stack our board a little more in our favor, then—"

A pager clipped to Howser's belt bleated two times in quick succession. The general unhooked it and scanned the digital readout of the name and number of the person calling.

"Tewkneda," he murmured to Greason, giving the name of their Soviet contact. "Better see what she wants."

"You can call from my office," Greason said.

They went up to the second floor, where Greason's office had a large plate-glass window overlooking the main room of the warehouse. He lit a cigarette and stared out at the work crews while Howser put through the call. It turned out to be a short, one-sided conversation, with Howser doing most of the listening. From what little he heard, however, Greason could tell that there had been some kind of snag in the master plan.

"So?" he asked when Howser hung up the phone. "What's up?"

"Tewkneda's being called back to Moscow," Howser said.

"Shit," Greason cursed. "Where does that leave us?"

"Hopefully everything will still be a go," Howser said. "Her replacement is already here. We'll meet him tomorrow. His name's Levdroko."

6

Oleg Levdroko had been in the States for years, working his way through the party ranks to head of the San Francisco desk of the KGB's First Department of the Foreign Directorate. But it was only during the past year that he had finally crossed paths with Able Team. There had been two incidents, each demonstrating the Russian's diabolical brand of genius, as well as his uncanny ability to enact his schemes from the sidelines so as to avoid capture.

Tanned from a long stay in Albuquerque, during which he'd grown a beard and moustache, Levdroko had also dyed his hair dark brown and gained weight, courtesy of a newfound resemblance to the pasty-faced bureaucrat he'd been back in San Francisco. The Russian's superiors had recently removed him from his former position in the wake of an unsuccessful mission, and it was only because of his long record of commendable service and the intervention of a former colleague in the Politburo that he hadn't been recalled to Moscow. Instead, he had a new lease on life and was even relishing the return of his former position as a field agent. After so many years of depending upon the competence of others for his reputation, his actions alone would again define his fate. Each mission would be his to run, and he would delegate authority only out of choice and not necessity.

Morning found him at Florissant Fossil Beds National Monument, just a short ride north of Rayford's Creek. He stood off by himself, barely within earshot of a tour guide telling her group the history of the plant and wildlife preserved throughout the area millions of years ago by a thin strata of shale. Staring out at the vast acres of wilderness, Levdroko could see the occasional stump of petrified sequoia. Just as surely as the fossils confirmed the likelihood that man, like most creatures upon the planet, would one day fade from prominence, they also demonstrated that there were ways for one's legacy to survive far into the future. For a man who had learned five months ago that a small lump at the base of his skull was an inoperable brain tumor, such lofty thoughts were not uncommon. Oleg Levdroko was very much concerned about the legacy he would leave behind.

A damn good agent. That's how he wanted to be remembered. Oleg Levdroko, who shunned his deathbed that he might serve his country one last time. Oleg Levdroko whose swan-song mission would become the stuff of legends, making him the inspiration to those agents who would follow him.

"Yes," he murmured to himself, smiling thinly. "A modest dream."

His reverie was interrupted by a sudden sensation of pain centered deep within his skull, radiating out in all directions like shock waves from an explosion. He winced and closed his eyes, shuddering as the wave of agony washed across his entire system, forcing him to lean against a nearby wall for support. He slowly drew in a deep breath, willing himself to rise above the pain. Think of something else, he told himself. The soft flesh of a woman...chilled vodka over ice with a splash of tonic...Prokofiev's Symphony No. 1 in compact disc...yes, all that together in a private suite decorated with lavish art treasures from around the globe. Never mind the pain. Imagine that woman. She is tall, white skin, almost translucent and so smooth to the touch. She has green eyes, sultry and inviting, soft full lips that glisten in the light of the fireplace....

"Oleg?"

The fantasy fled Levdroko's mind, leaving behind a remnant of the pain as he turned and saw that Karla Tewkneda was standing beside him. She was also in her early fifties, though she could easily pass for a woman much younger. She was simply dressed so that she resembled any other tourist at the site. When she wanted to, however, Levdroko knew that she could dress in the highest fashion and hold her own among the wealthiest aristocrats or businessmen. It was, after all, one of the main ways she'd managed to thrive so successfully as one of the KGB's top agents working undercover in the States.

"Oleg? Are you all right?"

Levdroko nodded. He had told no one of his tumor and he wanted to keep it that way. "I'm fine," he told her. "Just a small headache."

"It's a nice morning for a walk, yes?" the woman suggested.

"Yes, it is."

Levdroko fell in step beside Tewkneda and they strolled casually from the parking lot to a narrow path that led into a section of the park where tourists were allowed to wander. Neither of them spoke until they were well beyond earshot of the nearest visitors.

"You arrived sooner than I expected," the woman finally said.

"I came as soon as I was called," Levdroko countered modestly. "I can appreciate urgency."

"Yes, I suppose you can," Tewkneda said. "You must have contended with your share of it in San Francisco."

Levdroko turned and gazed coolly at the woman. "San Francisco was a long time ago."

Tewkneda smiled and nodded. "Of course. Forgive me. Better I should congratulate you on the work you've done in New Mexico. The reports have all been glowing."

"Thank you."

Tewkneda wasn't exaggerating, either. In the matter of a few short months, Levdroko had orchestrated a major infiltration into the heart of an Albuquerque computer firm that did extensive work for eleven separate defense contractors based along New Mexico's heralded high-tech corridor between Santa Fe and the

Texas border. The information had proved invaluable to KGB analysts, and the nature of the operation made Levdroko the ideal candidate to take over for Tewkneda in Colorado.

"I understand you're returning to Moscow," Levdroko told the woman. "Good news, I trust."

"A promotion," she responded, making it clear she had no intention of going into more detail.

Veering from the path, the couple sat down at one of the tables set around a small picnic area adjacent to the park. Tewkneda removed a deck of cards and began idly shuffling them. After Levdroko cut the deck, Tewkneda dealt gin hands to both of them, and as they played she brought him up-to-date on the assignment she'd been involved with for the past six months. Though he might have looked bored to anyone watching from a distance, Levdroko was listening attentively, committing each word to memory. He'd already read some briefs on the mission during his train ride from Albuquerque to Denver, and for the most part Tewkneda answered the more obvious questions that had come to mind.

"And with Cosvie gone and the Mountland merger a mere formality, we're on the verge of a major breakthrough," the woman concluded. With a vague smile she added, "And I'm going down with six...."

She laid out her hand. Levdroko had a play off two of her suits but was still left with two face cards. As he jotted down the score on a scrap of paper, he said, "What about the witnesses?"

"The two men are dead," Tewkneda responded casually as she gathered up the cards and handed them to Levdroko so he could deal.

"And the young girl?"

The woman shook her head. "She's been something of a problem."

"Oh? In the brief it said that we had an insider with the county sheriff's department."

"We do," Tewkneda said. "But she's not in their custody anymore."

"No?"

Tewkneda sighed and quickly related the circumstances behind Randall Howser's second failed attempt to silence Pamela Callahan, adding, "The men on the special task force must have realized there was a turncoat with county, so during the night they stole out with the woman. We aren't sure where they might have taken her, but we have plenty of connections throughout the state, so they won't get far."

"You have descriptions of these men?"

Tewkneda nodded. As she gave Levdroko the descriptions, he felt his pulse quicken. No, it couldn't be, he thought to himself. It's too much of a coincidence. But when she'd finished, he knew there could be no mistake.

"You know them?" she asked him.

"Possibly," he confessed as he began to deal the cards. "If I do, then I also have another reason to make sure this assignment succeeds. I owe them, and I want so very badly to repay my debt."

7

"Thanks again, but I still can't believe you did it!"

"Why not?"

"I don't know... for starters because it's like breaking the law, I guess."

"Well, whoever spilled the beans about where you were staying wasn't exactly playing by the rules, so I figure we're even."

Pamela and Blancanales had just climbed off the snowmobile that had brought them to a remote ranger's cabin deep in the heart of Rocky Mountain National Park. It was the tail end of the off-season, and no one had bothered to clear the snow off the service roads, although it was more than four miles to the nearest inhabited section of the park. Their isolation was far more assured than it had been in Salida.

After receiving a call from Lyons the previous evening, Hal Brognola had pulled the necessary strings to make the cabin available as an alternative safe house for Pamela. To get her there without alerting the county sheriff's people had been a tricky proposition, requiring a few diversionary tactics and some blatant deception. Grimaldi and Lyons had roused Allanson and the bald man in the middle of the night, leading them on a wild-goose chase after Schwarz, who had played the part of an interloper at the hotel. The ruse had worked, and while the chase was on, Pol had helped Pamela slip away, making their getaway in the rental car Grimaldi had secured at the airport.

A few hours on the road had brought them to their assigned rendezvous point near a ranger station just outside Grand Lake. While Pamela had waited in the car to avoid detection, Blancanales had gone into the station and, using the cover story concocted by Brognola, secured the snowmobile and the key to the remote cabin. As far as the Park Service was concerned, Blancanales and Pamela were research scientists for the Interior Department heading up to the high ground to check hibernation patterns of wildlife in the park.

Even though the morning sun had begun to push up above the taller peaks of the Continental Divide, the high-altitude temperature was still below freezing. The first thing they did after entering the cabin was to start a fire in the huge stone hearth taking up most of the north wall. As flames began devouring dry chunks of pine in the fireplace and generating heat, Pamela went into the adjacent bedrooms and unpacked a few personal items she'd been able to pack prior to fleeing the Depot Inn. There hadn't been much time to put together many other provisions, but the cabin pantry was reasonably stocked with canned goods and other nonperishables.

When Pol returned after going back to start up the power generator, Pamela came out of the room and joined him by the fire. As they warmed their hands before the flames, she asked him, "How long do you figure I'll have to stay here?"

"Dunno," he confessed. "But until we can figure out why you're in danger and who's behind it, it's best that you stay here."

"I know," she said sadly. Going over to the main window, she drew back the shades. Light spilled, revealing a majestic view of the backcountry. Staring out the window, she went on, "I wonder if I'm not just trading one prison for another, no matter how beautiful."

"I have a feeling it won't be more than a few days," Blancanales told her. "A week, tops."

Pamela shook her head and looked back at Pol. "But what about my uncle's funeral. And the movie?"

"I don't know what to tell you, Pam."

"It's not fair, damn it!" A tear stole down her cheek as she ran a finger along the cold glass. "None of this is fair."

Blancanales watched Pamela from across the room, and the way the light was falling on her, he clearly saw a hint of the way she'd looked years ago, back in East Los Angeles. He even remembered one time when he'd been working on his father's car and she'd been playing hide-and-seek with his sisters in the yard. Pamela had crawled too far underneath the front porch and had struck her forehead on a large support beam, giving herself a huge egg-size bruise. She'd come out crying, and while his sisters had gone off to get her uncle, Pol had stayed with Pamela and tried to calm her down. He remembered what he'd told her back then, and he repeated the advice to her now.

"Tough break, kiddo, but you know what your uncle would say."

Pamela glanced over her shoulder at Pol, obviously remembering the incident, as well. She blinked back her tears and smiled. "When the going gets tough, the tough get going."

"That's the spirit."

Pamela moved away from the window and wandered to the small kitchen area in the corner of the main room. She took down a can of soup from the adjacent pantry and opened it on the counter. As she poured the contents into a saucepan and set it over a low flame on the gas range, she glanced back at Pol.

"You know, I had a crush on you back then."

"What?" Pol said with a laugh.

"I knew you didn't notice," she said. "But that time, I didn't stop crying because of some saying of my uncle's. I just didn't want you to think I was a wimp."

"No . . . you're kidding."

"God's truth," Pamela replied. "But it was just a crush, of course. I got over it when school started."

Blancanales pretended to pout. "Oh, I see. . . ."

"I had to be realistic," she told him. "You were beyond reach, and besides, you probably only saw me as just another one of your sisters' little snot-nosed friends."

Blancanales made a face. "Snot-nosed?"

"You know what I mean."

Before Pol could answer, they both heard the drone of a motor drowning out even the high-pitched whine of the generator. It seemed to be coming from directly over their heads. Pamela's eyes widened with sudden terror and she shrank from the stove.

"Oh no," she cried. "They found us already!"

Pol calmly sauntered to the window. "Not to worry," he said as he glanced out. "It's not the 'they' you were thinking of."

Pamela joined him near the window and breathed a sigh of relief when she saw Schwarz and Lyons climbing out of a five-seat Bell chopper commandeered by Jack Grimaldi. The helicopter was idling in a clearing thirty-five yards from the cabin, and after Grimaldi shut off the rotors, he jumped down to the ground and helped the others remove three large wooden crates from the storage compartment.

"What are they bringing?" Pamela wondered aloud.

"A little something to help you pass the time here," Blancanales said, heading for the front door. "Come on, let's give them a hand."

Pamela held open the door as Blancanales headed out and helped the other men lug in the huge crates. They were clearly marked with stenciled descriptions of their contents.

"Editing equipment?" Pamela gasped incredulously. "What on earth?"

"We would have brought yours," Schwarz said, "but it would have alerted anyone casing your place out. It's the same make, though, isn't it?"

Pamela nodded as she glanced over the crates, which the men set down on the floor near the kitchen area. "This is wonderful . . . but I don't have anything to edit. My film's still back at my apartment, and the new reels are still at the developers, so—"

"Guess again," Grimaldi said, prying open one of the crates and showing Pamela five different canisters filled with film.

"My movie!" Pamela said. "But how . . . ?"

"Very discreetly," Lyons confessed. "Between sneaking into your apartment and getting the new stuff from the developers, we used all the training we've gotten in dirty tricks."

"I can't thank you enough!" Pamela said. "You have no idea how much this means to me."

"No problem," Schwarz said modestly.

Pamela turned to Blancanales. "You knew all about this, didn't you?"

Pol smiled. "What's that other saying—'the show must go on.'"

Lao Ti FINISHED the last of her steak, then leaned back in the chair and pushed the plate away from her.

"Wonderful," she told the others. "It brings back memories."

"Good ones, I hope," Brognola said.

"You know they are," the woman told her former boss. "I wouldn't trade the times I had here for anything."

"We've missed you," Kissinger said. They were in the dining room, with Aaron Kurtzman rounding out the foursome.

Kurtzman asked her, "Do you ever think of coming back?"

Lao Ti smiled diplomatically. "I think we had this discussion out in California a few months ago. My answer hasn't changed."

"We're a nice place to visit, but you wouldn't want to live here," Brognola teased.

"I didn't put it that way," she said. "I like my job in Pasadena. It's a good opportunity for me."

"Well, we're happy for you, then," Kurtzman said. "But can you stay on a few days before you head back?"

"I'd love to," the woman responded.

One of the security guards appeared in the doorway, interrupting the post-dinner chat. "Sir?" he called out to the chief. "Phone for you. Washington. They say it's urgent."

"They always say it's urgent," Brognola complained good-naturedly as he rose from the table and excused himself. While he was gone, the others fell into a discussion of Able Team, with Kissinger mentioning the assignment in Colorado and its possible connection to Oleg Levdroko. Lao Ti was familiar with the KGB agent from his involvement in the Yellow River Brigade's attempt to trigger earthquakes in California.

"Why do they think he's resurfaced in Colorado?" Lao Ti asked.

"Actually, from all we've been able to gather, most of the facts seem to indicate that he's been in New Mexico," Kurtzman answered. "Word is he's out from behind the desk now, doing field work—good stuff, too, at least as far as the Soviets are concerned."

"In other words, he's avoided elimination for failing in California," Lao Ti said.

"You could put it that way, yeah," Kissinger interjected.

"And how do you have him going from New Mexico to Colorado?"

"Couple of things," Hal Brognola said as he reentered the room in time to hear Lao Ti's question. He sat back down and withdrew a cigar from his shirt pocket, trimming it with a pair of small, stainless-steel scissors. "That was our contact with the CIA on the phone," he explained. "Their people in Moscow have confirmed that the KGB's doing some major juggling of personnel west of the Mississippi. The theory is that ever since that incident last month they want to avoid letting agents become too entrenched in one area. Anything they lose in efficiency they must figure they'll make up in reduced graft."

"Not the way I'd run things," Kurtzman said.

"Well, you're not KGB," Brognola told him. "Anyway," he went on, "the theory they have is that

Levdroko's been shifted up to Colorado to take the place of another agent they're pulling overseas."

"And what's going on in Colorado?" Lao Ti said.

"That," Brognola said, "is what we're hoping our boys will find out."

PAMELA HAD ALREADY put together more than a half hour of completed film for the documentary featuring her uncle, and although she had shot another fifteen minutes the day before Bones Callahan died, she figured that she'd only end up using a small fraction of the new footage in readying the movie for the festival.

While Lyons and Grimaldi pulled sentry duty outside the cabin, Blancanales and Schwarz were inside with Pamela, watching her carefully run film through the editing machine, pinpointing the places where she would make her editing cuts. Glancing over the woman's shoulder, both men could see the image of Bones Callahan panning for gold at the edge of the mountain stream.

"The screen's kind of small, but it looks like everything turned out okay," Pol observed.

"Thanks," Pamela said. "The lighting's a little off for what I had in mind, but I think I can juggle a few other scenes to make it work... Oh, here, you have to take a look a this."

As the men watched, Pamela adjusted the speed of the film's advance, capturing Bones's movements in slow motion. Finishing panning, he waded out of the stream and started climbing up a few boulders to the top of the embankment. Halfway up, he slipped on one of the rocks, clearly losing his balance. No doubt realizing he was still on camera, Bones kept a straight face and pretended he hadn't slipped at all, but was merely starting to dance. Exaggerating each move, the prospector pranced clumsily from rock to rock like a drunken ballerina, finally kicking off with both feet and landing on the embankment with the finesse of a paratrooper whose feet had fallen asleep on him. It was only then that he acknowledged the camera, grinning mischievously as he stretched his arms outward and bowed as if taking a curtain call.

"Funny guy," Schwarz murmured.

"Yes, he was," Pamela said, tears glimmering in her eyes as she froze the last frame of the sequence on the screen.

Blancanales felt a tightness in his throat, as well, recalling the many times that he'd witnessed the cheerful antics of Bones Callahan. To see him on film, so vitally alive, and know that in reality he was now laid out in some mortuary was a bittersweet sensation. Pol rested a hand on Pamela's shoulder and told her, "I've got a feeling that's the way he'd want to be remembered."

Pamela nodded, reaching for a facial tissue to dry her eyes. "I'll add this to the reel of outtakes," she said with a smile. "I've got a good six minutes of him clowning around."

After marking off the footage for future reference, Pamela resumed viewing the rest of the roll. There was an abrupt cut to a different location, showing Bones as he led his pack mule up a mountain path.

"Actually, this is going to end up being at the start of the documentary," Pamela explained. "I have a little theme music I'll record over this, and if I have time I'll superimpose the credits over... Oh, no!"

"What?" Blancanales asked.

"I was afraid of this," Pamela muttered, slowing the film down again. "Look up in the background, right near the top of the ridge...."

Both Pol and Schwarz leaned closer to the editing screen as Pamela adjusted the focus. Although it was barely noticeable at first glance, they were finally able to detect activity along the ridgeline. It looked like two men with shovels.

"Damn it," Pamela swore lightly, shaking her head in frustration. "I can't believe I didn't notice them in the frame."

"Who are they?" Schwarz asked.

"A couple of bikers," Pamela said, going on to recount the chance encounter and the way the two men had come down to talk with her and Bones before the park ranger had come by. She suddenly stopped herself and looked at Pol. They were both thinking the same thing.

"Harley's aren't really dirt bikes," Blancanales said. "And I don't know that many bikers who pan for gold as a hobby."

"And that person that tried to shoot me in Salida," Pamela said, "he got away on a motorcycle."

Blancanales nodded. "Bingo."

Pamela turned ashen as she looked back at the editing screen. "You think they killed my uncle?"

"It's worth considering."

"But why?"

Blancanales peered closely at the illuminated image on the small screen. "We need a better look at him," he said. "This film will fit in that projector we brought along, won't it?"

"Yes," Pamela said. "Of course."

"Good," Pol said. "Let's try it that way, okay?"

It took a few minutes to set up the projector and thread through the film. The Team hadn't bothered bringing a screen, so Schwarz improvised by taking a sheet off one of the beds and tacking it as tautly as possible to the paneled wall across from the fireplace. Pol drew the shades, making the cabin as dark as possible. Then the three of them watched carefully as Pamela switched on the projector and sped the film through to the sequence they were concerned about. The image on the sheet was more than three times larger than the one they'd been able to view on the editing screen, and it was easier to see what the men on the ridgeline were doing.

"You're sure they told you they were trying to dig something up?" Pol asked.

"Yes," Pamela said. "Uncle Bones caught a glimpse of them just before I shut off the film, and that's what he thought, too."

"Can you play it back again?" Blancanales asked her. "In slow motion this time."

"Sure."

She rewound the film to where the bikers first appeared, then reset the play button and slowed down the speed.

"Keep a close watch on the guy on the right," Pol said. "Especially on his shovel."

Schwarz walked a couple of steps closer to the screen, trying to get a better look. "I see," he said. "The shovel's full to begin with."

"Exactly," Pol said. "He's not trying to dig something up."

"What do you mean?" Pamela asked.

Pol turned to her. "I think the reason they came down to talk to you was because you filmed them burying something...."

"No...."

"And, unless I miss my guess, that's why your uncle was killed and why they're trying to get you, too."

8

After punching out for the day, Erica Leicar filed her time card and veered off to a small alcove to buy a cup of coffee. She took her time, trading a few words with the other maids at the Happy Trails Hotel, a forty-one-room complex situated just off the interstate between Denver and Colorado Springs. Lighting up a cigarette in the hallway, she made a quick call to her roommate while she finished the coffee, then went into the small change room she shared with the other female employees. She'd hoped the other would have already left, but one co-worker, Davina, was still there, weeping quietly as she changed out of her uniform.

"What's the matter now, Davina?" Erica asked as she stepped out of her work shoes and began fumbling with the combination lock on her locker. "Kirk giving you a hard time again?"

Davina nodded, dabbing at her eyes with a handkerchief. "He can be such a bastard!"

"I keep telling you you should find yourself someone better."

"But how?"

"Look around, that's how," Erica told the other woman. "Check out the bars some weekend. Join a health club. Get out of the house once in a while. *Capiche?*"

Davina smiled fragilely. "You make it sound so easy."

"It is easy," Erica said, taking off her uniform so she could change into jeans and a Denver Broncos T-shirt. "Trust me, it works."

"Is that how you met Randall?"

"You bet," Erica said. It was her turn to smile. "Seven weeks ago this Friday."

"He's a real hunk," Davina said.

"I know," Erica said, dragging a brush through her long, henna-tinted hair. "And there's plenty more where he came from, so do yourself a favor and go find somebody who'll make you forget Kirk, all right?"

Davina closed her locker with exaggerated determination. "Okay, I'll try it! He's away this weekend, so I'll hit the town Friday and Saturday!"

"That's the spirit," Erica coaxed. "Prime time. Go for it."

"Would you come with me?" Davina asked, pausing in the doorway. "You know, kinda coach me along...."

Erica eyed Davina from head to toe and shook her head. "You've got everything it takes except self-confidence. Listen, spend some time in front of the mirror before you go, okay? Tease the hair a little, slap some more mascara around the eyes, try some bright red on the lips . . . you'll do fine.''

"You really think so?"

"I guarantee it."

"Thanks, Erica. I appreciate it."

"My pleasure."

Once Davina had left, however, Erica rolled her eyes and sneered. "Get a life, ditzo."

Finally alone in the room, Erica quickly went through her uniform pockets until she found what looked like a piece of chewed gum wadded up in its original foil. Erica knew the wrapper actually contained a few lines worth of cocaine that she'd pinched from a baggie one of the lodgers had poorly hidden inside his room. She knew the amount wouldn't be missed, and there would be enough to get both her and Randall high and still have some left over to sell for a profit. Not a bad racket at all. In the four months she'd been working as a maid at the Happy Trails, Erica figured she must have stumbled onto close to a dozen such finds, which she liked to think of as fringe benefits for having to suffer the indignity of cleaning up after other people.

After sampling a quick snort, Erica rewrapped the coke and tucked it inside her bra, and not a moment too soon. Another of the maids came in, cursing about someone who'd broken the mirror in their room. Erica excused herself and hurried out of the hotel, aware that she was running a few minutes late. If there was one thing she'd learned about Randall, it was that he hated to be kept waiting.

He was at their appointed rendezvous spot, a hot dog stand halfway down the street. Astride his Harley, Randall was wolfing down the last of his second chili dog. Seeing Erica, he tossed the rest of the dog into the dirt and jumped on his kickstart, rousing the Sportster to life. From the way he revved the engine as she strided up to him, Erica knew he was in a bad mood. Better think quick, girl, she told herself, knowing that Randall had a way of taking out his frustrations on her.

"It took me a couple of extra minutes," she told him as she climbed onto the bike behind him and kissed his ear, "but it was worth it. I got us some candy."

"Good," he grunted over the drone of his engine. "I need it."

She hugged him, letting one hand trail down near his groin. "That's not all you need, I bet. Let's go to your place and I'll take your mind off things for a while. Okay?"

By way of reply, Randall eased his left hand off the clutch, forcing the Harley forward with so much momentum the front wheel swung up into the air. Erica grimaced as Randall leaned back into her, balancing the bike on one wheel for a full twenty-five yards. Once the front wheel touched back down, Randall opened the throttle wider and they sped down the access road to the highway, taking the southbound entrance ramp toward Colorado Springs.

"What's the matter?" she asked above the engine's roar and the howl of wind in her ears. He didn't answer her, and she was forced to hold on tightly as he weaved through traffic for the next two miles, then veered off at the next exit. Randall had become increasingly moody the past couple of weeks, and Erica found herself wondering if by appeasing him she was just putting off an inevitable rejection. For all her impatience with Davina's tales of romantic woe, Erica knew that her own situation wasn't all that much better. Sure, she and Randall had great times when they were high and making out, but once the party was over, there wasn't much intimacy to get them through the more sober moments. Maybe, she thought, she should start following her own advice and look for someone else.

Oreville was one of the newest bedroom communities sprouting off the interstate north of Colorado Springs, and Hamstead Acres was the most prestigious division within the town. It's large, sprawling lots and custom-built homes started in the seven hundred thousand dollar range. Most residents entered the tract through a marbled gateway off Ray Avenue, but Randall preferred the back way, which wound up through the foothills and circled behind the homes. Halfway around, Randall slowed down and left the road, forcing Erica to hold tight again as he guided the Harley over rugged terrain to the back of his father's property. Buck lived in the main house, a lavish, four-story affair surrounded by 120-year-old pines. A guest cottage more than a hundred yards away had been built amid a stand of aspens that glittered in the midday sun. Since returning to Colorado fifteen months ago after eight years of eking out a hand-to-mouth existence in San Francisco, Randall had called the cottage home. Now, however, it seemed as if that was about to change.

"What the hell?" Randall shouted as he brought the Harley to a stop in the driveway leading to the cottage. He turned off the ignition and stared dumbfoundedly at his father, who was on his way out of the guest house, carrying an armload of clothes and record albums.

"What's going on?" Randall called out as he climbed off his bike, inadvertantly elbowing Erica in the ribs. His eyes were on Buck and he didn't bother to apologize.

"What the hell does it look like?" Buck shot back as he unceremoniously dumped his son's belongings in the back of an old green Chevy pickup parked in front of the cottage. "You're out of here, as of right now."

"Hey, man, you're joking, right?"

Without warning, Buck suddenly whirled around, lashing out at his son with a reasonable facsimile of the right uppercut that had won him a few ribbons during his days in the service. Randall took the blow on the chin and staggered back, nearly toppling over his bike. Erica caught him and held him up while he struggled to regain his balance.

"How's that for a joke, shit-for-brains?" Howser railed at his son. "You want another punchline?"

"Don't talk to him like that!" Erica blurted out, glaring at the older man.

"I'll talk to my damn son any damn way I feel like, princess." Howser took a step forward, holding out the key to the pickup truck. "If you're so anxious to do him a favor, drive his shit to your place and then come back to get what's left of him after I'm through."

"If I go, he goes with me," Erica said, barely able to believe what she was saying. Even as she was defending Randall, she was cursing herself for doing it.

"No," Howser insisted. "You leave him here. We have some things to discuss, man to man...."

Randall managed to stand up unassisted and he shook Erica's hand away from him. His chin was already beginning to swell where he'd been struck. "I'm okay, damn it. Go on, beat it," he said, talking to Erica although his eyes were focused on his father. "I can handle myself."

"You're sure?" Erica said uncertainly.

"I said beat it!"

Erica reluctantly took the keys and climbed into the pickup. Once the engine turned over, she carefully backed up, making sure she steered wide of the Harley on her way out.

Alone, father and son faced off.

"You blew your last chance with me, kid. I want you out of here."

"Hey, I've done some decent jobs for you," Randall countered, meeting his father's gaze unflinchingly. "I saved your ass with that corporal, I iced Cosvie and those two guys who saw us burying the body. So what's the big deal blowing a gasket just because that skirt's got Lady Luck on her side."

"I don't believe in luck," Howser said coldly. "I believe in rewarding failure just as strongly as I reward competence."

"You don't have to kick me out of here," Randall insisted. "Shit, give me one more crack at her and she's history."

Howser shook his head. "You're the one that's history, kid. I never liked you from the start, and you've screwed up your whole life. I'm done bailing you out."

Randall's face reddened with rage. "With all your support," he shouted sarcastically, "it's no wonder I failed. Of course, my dear brother—"

"Leave him out of this," Howser warned. "This doesn't have anything to do with him."

"Bullshit. Everything's always got something to do with him."

"Keep it up and I'll give you a left to go with that right."

Randall reached to his waist, unsnapping the clasp on an eight-inch-long buck knife. He grabbed the hilt and pulled the weapon out, letting the sun glint off its stainless-steel blade. "Go ahead," he taunted his father. "Try it! I'll carve your fingers into French fries!"

Buck calmly regarded the knife in Randall's hand. "Oh, so that's the way you want to play, is it?"

"I ain't playing, old man. I'll cut you!"

"That so?" Howser reached behind his back, coming up with a Colt Cobra Model D-3 pistol. As he nonchalantly aimed the gun at his son's chest, he drawled, "I've got six little friends that say you won't."

Randall glanced down the barrel pointed his way, doing his best not to show his fear. He kept his knife held out before him. Neither man spoke for some time, then Randall finally muttered, "Why'd you always have it in for me, huh? What'd I ever do to rate such a shit for an old man?"

"You were born," Howser told him. "I was fed up with your mother and ready to get her out of my life when you had to come along. Sick all the time as a kid, whining and crying. I never could stand the sight of you."

Randall's jaw stiffened. In a flash of rage he pulled back his hand and was about to hurl the knife at his father when the Cobra sounded with a loud blast. A 200-grain slug slammed into the knife, glancing off the blade and drawing blood as it ripped through the fleshy back of Randall's hand. Dropping the weapon, the younger man recoiled in pain. Howser stepped forward and kicked the knife off the driveway, then took aim at his son again.

"Not that you deserve it, but I'll let you live," he said. "Just get out of my sight. Go run back to your mother in San Francisco. Or, better yet, go join your biker buddies and get your ass splattered on the highway some night when you're out joyriding. It'll save me that ten grand a year I've been pumping into your trust fund."

Cupping his wound with his other hand, Randall backed away. When he reached his bike, he untied a red bandanna from his backrest and used it to staunch the flow of blood. Then, straddling the Harley, he started up the engine and stared one last time at his father.

"You'll pay," he promised, "I'll make you pay!"

"Yeah, yeah, talk big." Howser chuckled. He aimed lazily at the bike, blowing away one of the rearview mirrors. "Just remember something. You come up against me again, I'll rub you out so fast you won't have time to juice your jeans."

Randall ignored the taunt and sped off, heading the way Erica had gone in the pickup. He blinked as the wind pushed past his face, rousing a few tears loose from the corners of his eyes.

9

Although they took care to avoid the tourist congestion at Gold Rush Daze, Lyons and Grimaldi were still close enough to the site to see employees wearing black armbands in memory of Bones Callahan.

"Kinda get the idea he was well liked, huh?" Grimaldi said as he hiked up the same mountain path that had led Callahan to his doom two days before.

"Yeah," Lyons said, "but there was obviously somebody who didn't care for him."

"Maybe so," Grimaldi said, "but remember, the way it looks now, he was killed only because he was at the wrong place at the wrong time. The odds are those bikers didn't even know him personally."

"Doesn't make him any less dead, does it?" Lyons muttered with disgust.

Both men were wearing Levi's, hiking boots, flannel shirts and bulky leather vests that helped conceal their shoulder holsters and Government Model automatics. Pamela had given them directions to Bones's favorite stomping grounds after the Team had decided to investigate the area in hopes of unearthing some clues that had gone unnoticed by the authorities. It didn't take long before they came upon the base of a fifty-foot-wide swath of destruction scarring the hillside. Countless tons of loose rock and gravel lay where it had come to a rest after its downhill slide. It didn't take much imagination to realize the force such an avalanche must have packed.

"We won't bother checking the whole slide," Lyons said, plotting strategy as he looked over the hillside. "Let's just check around the stream where Bones and that other guy got nailed, then trace the slide up to where it started."

"I don't know, Ironman," Grimaldi said as he started walking uphill. "I think we'd have a better chance of finding a needle in a haystack than stumbling onto anything here. Especially if there was a mole with the sheriff's department during the first sweep."

"You're probably right," Lyons said. "But we have to at least give it a shot."

The path leading to the stream where Callahan and the older prospector had died was half-buried in rubble, and it was difficult for the two men to traverse the obstruction. Their footing was precarious, and on several occasions the larger rocks they used for support gave way under their weight, triggering new, smaller slides. Finally they managed to reach the stream but because it had been partially blocked by the avalanche, it had backed up and overflown its banks, creating a small, waist-deep pond where it had once been a shallow creek.

"This is great," Lyons said cynically. "If there was any evidence, it's probably underwater by now."

The two men fanned out, eyes on the ground, using branches to prod rocks to one side and sweep gravel off sections of the path. In a way they felt as if they were prospectors looking for another sort of gold. After about ten minutes of looking, Lyons crouched down and pulled loose a flat pan mired in a mixture of gravel and mud. It was a prospecting pan, probably dented as much by years of use as by the slide. Turning it over, Lyons saw an inscription and brushed off some of the dirt so he could read it better.

"What's it say?" Grimaldi called out.

"'To Uncle Bones, with love from Pamela.'"

Lyons shook his head grimly as he took the pan to the edge of the pond and leaned over to rinse it off. By now the sun had passed above the treetops overhead, and when the first rays fell upon the pond, something in the water glinted and caught his eye.

"What do we have here?" he murmured to himself, setting aside the pan in favor of a long branch, which he used to reach into the cold depths of the pond. Grimaldi came over and watched as Lyons carefully poked the end of the stick near the object, which was fortunately lying in a newly formed part of the pond where there was no sediment to be stirred up.

"Looks like a camera," Grimaldi said.

"I think so," Lyons agreed. He managed to loop a short length of strap around the end of the stick, then carefully he worked the camera loose from the cluster of small rocks that had nearly buried it. Once he had it out of the water, Lyons swung the camera over to Grimaldi, who unslung it from the stick. There was an identification tag on the case.

"Bill Cincino," Grimaldi said. "He was the other guy killed in the slide, wasn't he?"

"Yeah."

Grimaldi closely scrutinized the camera. "Took a real beating and the lens is cracked. Nine shots taken."

"Any chance they could be developed?"

"Depends," Grimaldi said. "I don't know much about that, but my guess would be no."

"It's worth checking out," Lyons said.

Grimaldi nodded in agreement and wrapped the camera in a handkerchief, then tied it to his belt so he'd have both hands free. They spent another fifteen minutes searching the area without finding any more clues, then continued uphill, following the path created by the avalanche.

"One thing I still don't get," Grimaldi said as they walked. "If these bikers wanted to get rid of Callahan and his niece that badly, why didn't they do it the same day they saw them? It would have been a hell of a lot easier than all these other things they've had to do."

"Pamela said something about a couple of rangers driving by, remember," Lyons said. "I'm sure that had a lot to do with it."

"Yeah, probably."

The steeper the hill became, the more difficult it was for the men to follow the slide. They resorted to trail-blazing a series of switchbacks, veering back and forth on the harsh terrain. Again, it was a risky venture and they both were continually making sudden twists and turns and grabbing at shrubs and saplings to keep from tumbling downhill each time they lost their balance. The arduous climb finally brought them to a clifftop whose edge was lined with huge boulders except for the one gap where the landslide had started. After the men had paused long enough to catch their breath, they turned their attention to the lip of the precipice.

"I don't see any signs of tampering," Lyons said after squatting for a closer look where the huge boulders had once rested. "But, then, I'm sure that whoever initiated it took care not to leave any tracks."

"That's what I think," Grimaldi said, glancing around. "The ground around here looks like it was swept with a leafy branch."

"Not only that, but from up here you've got a clear view of the stream." Lyons pointed down at a distant pond. "All they had to do was wait for him to wander into the path, then start things rolling."

A more thorough search of the clifftop confirmed their hypothesis, as they finally came across a short length of exposed tire track from a motorcycle. Lyons checked the depth of the marking and said, "Deep tracks. Probably a couple of big guys doubling up on one bike."

"If you say so, Sherlock."

Lyons glanced over his shoulder at Grimaldi. "Cut me a little slack, okay?"

"Hey," the pilot countered. "I'm just trying to throw in a little comic relief, okay?"

"Yeah, well, I don't feel like yucking it up."

Lyons stood up and glanced at the nearest ridgeline, more than two hundred yards away. "That looks like where the bikers were digging. Let's go up there and wrap this up."

Before leaving the ranger's cabin, the men had taken Polaroid shots of certain frames from Pamela's film, and they were able to use the photographs to guide them to the site where the digging had taken place. It turned out to be a rugged, overgrown area thick with clumps of brush. Several of the bushes, however, looked less healthy than the others, and on closer inspection Lyons and Grimaldi saw that they had been uprooted and moved from their original location. Dragging them aside, the men found themselves staring at an oblong hole in the ground, half filled in with dirt.

"A grave," Lyons murmured.

Grimaldi knelt beside the indentation, using a stick to prod the soft earth. "Ex-grave."

"So that's it," Lyons said, seeing the puzzle fall into place. "Bones and his niece witnessed a burial they weren't invited to."

"And those bikers didn't want anyone to find out who was buried," Grimaldi surmised.

"It adds up that way for me," Lyons said. "Now we just have to figure out who was killed and who did the killing."

"Shit, and I thought we were making progress," Grimaldi grumbled.

For a third time in less than an hour, the two men once again threw themselves into a search, this time concentrating on the small confined area of the makeshift grave. More than a half hour later, the sum of the latest findings were a half-dozen human hairs and several scoops of dirt containing bits of dried blood.

"A lot of good this will do us," Grimaldi said.

"You might be surprised," Lyons said, taking care in the way he wrapped the items before slipping them into his vest pocket. "You know about genetic fingerprinting, don't you?"

Grimaldi nodded thoughtfully. "Maybe it'll work."

"Worth a shot, at any rate," Lyons said. "Come on, let's get out of here."

First they put the loose bushes back over the grave site. Then, rather than retrace their steps, the two men opted for a less demanding trail that took them wide of the slide area. They hadn't gone far, however, when Lyons suddenly veered off the trail and dragged Grimaldi along with him.

"What the—"

"Shh," Lyons hissed. "We got company...."

Crouching low behind the thick base of an ancient conifer, the two men peered down the trail, where they saw a man hiking toward them. He was wearing khaki hiking shorts and a loose-fitting parka. It wasn't until he paused for a moment and took off his wide-brimmed hat that Lyons and Grimaldi recognized him as the bald sheriff's officer who'd been watching over Pamela back at the Depot Inn in Salida. "What the hell's he doing here?" Grimaldi whispered. "Do you think he's on to us?"

"I'm not sure," Lyons confessed. "Hopefully he's just keeping an eye on things."

"But for who?" Grimaldi said. "The sheriff or the bikers?"

The bald man reached to his waist for a walkie-talkie, and after making a quick call, he wandered off the path and headed away from Lyons and Grimaldi.

"He's headed for the grave," Lyons said.

"That settles it," Grimaldi said. "He's gotta be the mole. I say we go take him aside for a little chat."

Lyons shook his head. "No. I've got a better idea." He took the wrapped hairs and blood samples and handed them to Grimaldi, telling him, "Go get this expressed to Bear somehow and have him run a trace on it, then take the camera back to the cabin. They've got the stuff there to develop the film if it's salvage-able."

"What are you going to do?"

Lyons glanced up at the bald man, who was now nosing around the ridgeline where they'd found the grave. "I'm going to stick to him and see where he'll lead me."

10

After four straight hours of slaving over the moviola, Pamela finally shut the machine off and pushed herself away from the kitchen table.

"I need a break," she groaned, rising from her chair and stretching.

"I've been trying to tell you that," Blancanales reminded her. "I can't believe you haven't ruined your eyes at that thing, not to mention your back."

"Well, the back's not doing so hot," Pamela confessed, kneading her stiff shoulders and neck muscles. "I'm a little tight."

"Come over here," Pol told her. He was sitting in an overstuffed chair facing the fireplace, where a healthy fire blazed. He motioned for Pamela to sit down on the rug with her back to him. "Okay, here's the deal," he told her. "You get a massage but it's gonna cost you."

"Uh-oh," Pamela said as she sat down. "What's your price?"

"Every other marshmallow," he told her.

"What?" she laughed.

"I was nosing around the pantry and found these," he told her, producing an unopened package of marshmallows. "They passed the squeeze test, but I figured they'd go stale in another week or so..."

"I bet you did," Pamela said. She took the coat hanger he handed her and bent it into a long prong capable of reaching the hearth flames from her sitting position. As she fit the first marshmallow on the tip and held it out, she went on, "I swear, Rosario, this is the first time I've done this since I left East L.A."

"It's been a while for me, too," Pol confessed. He reached out and place his large, callused hands on Pamela's shoulders. She moaned with relief the moment he began to massage.

"Oh, that is so wonderful."

"You need it," Pol said. "You're practically in knots."

"Been a hard week for me," she said.

"I know."

When the flame erupted on the surface of the marshmallow, Pamela quickly pulled it away and blew the fire out, leaving a brownish, charred shell. "Oops," she said. "I guess I'll take this one."

"No, I like 'em well-done," Pol said.

Looking over her shoulder, Pamela guided the marshmallow to Pol's waiting lips, leaving his hands free to continue massaging her. He carefully bit down and pulled the candy off with his mouth, then murmured contentedly as he chewed the white goo. "Perfecto!" he announced.

Pamela suddenly let out an uncontrolled burst of laughter and nearly dropped the fresh marshmallow she was skewering to the hanger.

"What's so funny?" Pol wanted to know.

"'Perfecto,'" she repeated, still laughing. "I remember you saying that one night when we were having these things over at my uncle's. Remember? It was, what, more than fifteen years ago?"

Pol shook his head. "Nope, must have been longer. You better refresh my memory."

"You were just back from Vietnam," Pamela recalled. "And Uncle Bones had your whole family over for a barbecue. I remember just staring at you all night, because it seemed like you'd aged so much those years you were away."

"I had," Pol told her, starting to remember the details of that gathering. It had been a wonderful time, just the kind of emotional tonic a returning vet needed. "Go on," he told Pamela as he stroked the back of her neck.

"Well, you hardly paid any attention to me all night . . . not that you ever did, mind you. And even though I figured you were now way too old for me, my pride was still at stake and I was determined that, one way or another, you were going to notice me."

Pol smiled. "It's beginning to come back to me, now."

"Let me finish. It was after supper, and I was roasting marshmallows for all the younger kids, scheming madly all the time for a way to get to you. I must have gotten carried away daydreaming, because the next thing I knew your sister Maria was pointing at the barbecue and crying because her marshmallow was being burned to a crisp.

"And what happens? You reach out and blow the flames out, then grab the marshmallow with your bare hands and pop it into your mouth, just to show Maria it was okay. You looked at her, then at me, and you said..."

"Perfecto." Pol chuckled.

"And you left right after that with Hector," Pamela said with a pout. "I was crushed."

"It was important," Pol told her. "He needed me."

"I know," she said, "but it still hurt."

"Sorry."

"Just tell me, when you said that...for whose benefit was it really? Mine or Maria's?"

"Both," he told her. "Honest."

As she held out the second marshmallow for toasting, Pamela leaned back, pressing her shoulder blades against Pol's knees and tilting her head back to look at him. "Did you like me any?"

"Of course," he told her. "I thought you were a great kid."

"Kid?"

"Well," he reminded her, "don't forget that to me you were just as real young as I was real old."

"And now...?"

Staring down into her eyes, Blancanales couldn't deny that there was a kind of attraction that was different from anything he'd felt all those years ago. This Pamela was not the childhood companion of his sisters, but a mature, beautiful woman, close at hand before a crackling, romantic fire. At any other time he knew what would happen next. He also knew that he couldn't let that happen now.

"Now I think you're really something special." He leaned forward and kissed her lightly on the forehead. "And if I wasn't a gentleman and we weren't grieving for your uncle, this all might lead to something we'd enjoy for the moment and regret later."

"Do you have to be so damn wise?" she said with a pout.

"Your marshmallow's overheating," Pol told her, easing her back to a sitting position and resuming his massage. She fetched the marshmallow and nibbled on it slowly. Neither of them spoke for the next few minutes, letting the sounds of the fire battle with the drone of the outdoor generator.

"What am I supposed to do about the funeral," Pamela finally said, breaking the silence between them. "I have to be there."

"The people who want you dead know that," Pol said.

"I don't care," she said with determination. "I'm going to be there. Please don't try to keep me away, Rosario."

Pol smiled. "I kinda figured you'd feel that way."

"I mean it, too."

"I know. And I'll make you a deal," he bartered. "I'll see that you get to the funeral, but you have to do me another favor."

"Name it."

"Stop calling me Rosario...."

AFTER CASING OUT THE HILLS where Bones Callahan had died and the mysterious grave had been dug, the bald man hiked down to Gold Rush Daze. Lyons was able to follow him from a distance until they reached level ground, where he had to make a decision whether to continue to hang back and risk losing the man in the crowd or close the gap between them and risk being spotted and recognized. With barely a moment's hesitation, Lyons forged ahead, cutting through a shallow wash that was thick with weeds and bramble. By the time both men entered the tourist site, they were less than sixty feet away from each other. In the crowded confines of the mock-up town, however, Lyons knew that he had to get even closer.

Pausing near one of the souvenir stands, Lyons saw that the bald man was taking aside employees and flashing his badge as he asked them questions. The fact that the other man was staying put momentarily bought Lyons some time, and he took advantage of it. Two booths down, Lyons saw that they were selling prospecting apparel, from flat pans and hip boots to wide-brimmed hats and fake beards. More than a few men mingled about in these costumes, and after purchasing a hat and beard, Lyons joined their ranks. He felt like an overage trick-or-treater, but the ploy was just quirky enough to work.

Threading his way through the crowd, Lyons inched closer to the bald man until finally less than ten feet separated them. The officer was at the petting zoo, talking to Emily, the last employee to have spoken to Bones and Pamela Callahan. Standing near a group of small children and watching them as if he were a father, Lyons overheard the man call himself Deputy Bedson. As Lyons suspected, the man was inquiring if Pamela had been by the site since Bones's death or if she had otherwise mentioned where she was staying prior to her uncle's funeral.

"No, I have no idea where she is," the woman said. "Hiding, I suspect."

"What makes you say that?" Bedson asked her.

"When they first brought the body down from the mountains," Emily explained, "I told Pamela how Bones had died in a freak accident. But she wouldn't accept that. She said she was sure her uncle had been murdered."

"Murdered?" Bedson looked puzzled. "Why would she have thought that?"

"I don't know for sure," Emily confessed. "I think maybe it was denial. She looked up to him so much, maybe she had trouble accepting that he could die in an accident. I don't know...."

"And you're sure you don't know where she is?"

Emily shook her head, a worried look coming to her face. "Why, has something happened to her? Was she right?"

Lyons saw the deputy smile indulgently. "I'm sure she's all right, ma'am. It's just that we have some paperwork that needs wrapping up, that's all."

"Well, if you want, I could have her give you a call if she comes by," Emily suggested.

"I don't think that's a good idea."

"Why not?"

Bedson shook his head and sighed. "Well, ma'am, I didn't want to have to bring this up, but we've learned that Ms Callahan is, well, emotionally disturbed."

"No?"

"Afraid so, ma'am. Paranoid schizophrenic, as I understand it." He looked at the woman with practised sincerity. "These delusions of persecution...it's not the first time she's had them."

Emily glanced over at the pets, sorting through her memory. She finally nodded, as if remembering something. "He always was saying how she was a special child. I didn't think he meant it literally, but now I can see it. The way he always doted over her so much."

"In any case," Bedson said, "if she should happen to show up, the absolute worst thing you could do is tell her we were looking for her. I mean, the odds are she hasn't been taking her medication."

"Medication?"

Bedson nodded. "For her condition. Look, ma'am," he said, giving her a business card, "if she does show up, could you do me a favor and try to detain her, or at least find out where she's staying. Then contact me. And only me."

Emily eyed the card and slipped it into her pocket. "Of course, I'll do what I can to help. That poor child."

"And I don't need to remind you to be discreet."

"I understand," Emily said.

Bedson exchanged a few parting words, then headed back into the crowd. Lyons, who had overheard most of the exchange, felt a burning rage rush through him, and he longed to take Emily aside and set her straight on the real situation behind Pamela's plight. Even more tempting was his desire to drag Bedson back up into the mountains and throttle him to within an inch of his life, regardless of whether or not he could get any information out of him. As a steeled professional, however, he knew that neither option would serve him better than sticking to the original plan, and he brought his patience under control as he left the petting zoo and followed Bedson to the parking lot.

Fortunately, Grimaldi had taken a shuttle bus from the site, leaving behind their rental car. Once he determined that Bedson was driving a late-model Suzuki Samurai, Lyons hurried to his Mustang, which was parked at the far end of the lot.

Pulling onto the road and holding his position six cars behind Bedson, Lyons took advantage of a palm-size communicator concealed under the front seat. An instrument of space-age sophistication, the communicator represented the ultimate tribute to the technological wizardry generated by the minds of Stony Man Farm. Built by Aaron Kurtzman with input from both Lao Ti and Gadgets Schwarz, the deceptively small device was capable of transmitting a high-powered scrambled signal to Pol Blancanales's communicator at the ranger's cabin, more than a hundred miles away, without risking interception via either telephone lines or conventional radio waves.

"What's up?" Pol asked Lyons, his voice sounding slightly muted over the small, thumb-size speaker built into the communicator.

Lyons described what little headway he'd made with Bedson and related the direction they were headed, then asked, "Have you heard from Grimaldi yet?"

"Yeah, he just checked in," Blancanales reported. "He's at a bus stop halfway to Denver. We can't help him with that film, but I had Bear do a quick computer run and track down a place in Denver that can help him out. He's going to take the shuttle there, then Schwarz will pick him up on the way back from the airport."

"Airport?" Lyons said, passing a few cars to stay closer to the Samurai as the speed limit rose. "Who's he picking up at the airport?"

"Old friend," Pol said. "Lao Ti."

"You're kidding!"

"Nope. She was out visiting at the Farm when I checked in. Between you and me, I think she was itching for a little action. I figured we could use her and asked if she'd be interested in giving us a few days. She said she'd be on the next plane."

"Sounds like her, all right."

"What's up on your end?" Blancanales queried.

"Nada," Lyons said. "As in nada thing."

"You still have your rotten sense of humor, so there's still hope."

"Hah hah." Keeping an eye on Bedson's Samurai, now directly ahead of him, Lyons said, "Why don't I give you a license number to run through the microchips. Who knows, maybe Bedson's other boss has title to it."

"Not likely, but let me have it anyway."

As Lyons was giving Pol the number, the Samurai's turn signal flashed on and Bedson switched lanes, heading for the next exit.

"Gotta go," Lyons said. "Might be on to something."

Signing off, Lyons exited from the highway, letting a few more cars get between him and Bedson again. The Samurai turned right at the first light and pulled into Rayford's Creek Savings, a sixty-foot trailer serving as an interim place of business while a more permanent building was under construction on the other side of the lot.

Bedson parked and pulled out an envelope from his pocket as he headed up the steps to the trailer. Lyons pulled into a gas station halfway down the block and kept an eye on the trailer as he raised Blancanales again on the communicator.

"Looks like he's cashing a check," Lyons said. "Let me give you the name of the place and see if Bear can't get into their records. Any luck, we can trace the check to some higher-ups."

BY NATIONAL STANDARDS Stapleton International was a new airport. But the rampant growth in Denver and the city's strategic location as a hub for cross-county flights had quickly made Stapleton an overtaxed, congested airfield where incoming jets were commonly stacked in holding patterns for extended periods while they waited for runway clearance. Unsurprisingly, therefore, it was more than an hour past its supposed arrival time that a Delta 747 from Washington finally touched down and taxied to its designated terminal.

Inside the terminal, Gadgets Schwarz got off the phone with Jack Grimaldi and went over to gate 25B, where dozens of other people were already gathered and waiting for the appearance of loved ones. Schwarz always felt uncomfortable in the face of such gatherings, most likely because they reminded him of what little intimacy he'd been allowed during his life. True, there were some fond memories of his youth in Pasadena, and he was as close to the men of Stony Man Farm as any brothers ever were, but he still felt a gnawing absence in his life. His recent trysts with Sandy Meisner had temporarily filled the void, but he had doubts that their relationship could ever be something that would evolve beyond an occasional get-together, as both of them were far more committed to their work.

His work. That was his life, and harsh as the price was for that almost single-minded devotion, he knew deep down that any other arrangement would leave him feeling even less fulfilled. Face it, he thought to himself as he scanned the faces of those pouring into the terminal from the jumbo jet, you can't have it all. Any luck and you get a chance to choose the game you play; beyond that, you just have to bear down and do the best with the cards you're dealt.

Lao Ti was among the last to leave the plane, and when she spotted Schwarz she smiled brightly and strode over to him. He kissed her lightly on the cheek as she gave him an embracing hug.

"It's so good to see you," she told him.

"Likewise," Schwarz said. "I understand we almost missed you."

Lao Ti nodded as they headed out of the terminal. She had all her things in a carry-on bag so they could avoid the baggage claim congestion. "I was just about to leave the Farm when Blancanales called. It sounded like you could use a little help and I was kind of homesick for the old times, so here I am."

"Welcome back aboard, even if it's only for a day or two."

"What's the latest?" she asked him once they reached the rental car Schwarz was driving. He brought her up to speed on the situation as they left the airport and headed down Quebec Street to the nearest shopping plaza, concluding, "Lyons is still trailing the bald man, but Grimaldi's back. I just talked to him. Pamela couldn't do anything about the film from that camera, but Jack called around and found a lab near that specializes in tricky cases. Any luck and he'll have some pictures when we pick him up."

When they pulled into the plaza, Grimaldi was standing in front of the photo shop, holding a small packet. Even before he got in the car, he flashed a thumbs-up.

"They turned out?" Schwarz asked him.

Grimaldi nodded as he patted Lao Ti on the shoulder and exchanged hellos. Then he told them, "All nine shots turned out, and three of them might be of use to us."

"How so?"

Grimaldi opened the packet and pulled out the snapshots in question. "Near as I can figure out, that guy must have had a run-in of some sorts with whoever was in this truck and he took their picture while they were driving off."

Lao Ti and Schwarz glanced at the photos, which were slightly out of focus and obviously taken in a hurry. All three shots featured a green pickup, in the back of which were two motorcycles.

"He just missed the license plate," Lao Ti noticed. "That's too bad."

"Yeah, but maybe we can narrow it down somehow," Grimaldi said hopefully. "And take a close look at the arm sticking out the window."

Schwarz held the photo close. "Looks like someone giving the finger."

"Yeah, but check out the forearm."

"A tattoo," Schwarz said. "Looks like a devil or something."

"It's not as good as a fingerprint, but maybe it'll help," Grimaldi said. "I sure as hell hope so, 'cause we could use a breakthrough."

11

Not now, Levdroko thought with a grimace. Not now.

But the agony persisted, rampaging through his skull like a fireball of white heat, making him dizzy and unleashing a chilled sweat across his brow. He closed his eyes, drawing in deep breaths, once again pitting his will against the pain. He was behind the wheel of a leased Mercedes, waiting at a traffic signal five miles from his destination. He checked the dashboard clock. 5:31. He was already late and caught in the middle of rush-hour traffic. There was no way he could not show up. Too much was at stake. But he couldn't let them see him like this, either. He had to be in control, to look worthy of command.

The sudden blare of a car horn snapped Levdroko to attention, forcing his eyes open. The light had changed to green. The driver behind was holding one hand on his horn and waving angrily at Levdroko with the other.

Levdroko eased his Mercedes through the intersection and pulled off to the curb, letting the other car pass. Once alongside the Mercedes, the other driver slowed down enough to get a good look at Levdroko.

"Asshole!"

Levdroko stared back at the man with a look of cold contempt. How easy it would be for him to reach inside his coat, pull out his Browning automatic and pump a few quick shots into that foul-mouthed bastard. Instead, however, Levdroko sat calmly and waited for the other car to move on before he pulled back out into traffic. As he had hoped, the rush of pain was short-lived, and by the time he reached the end of the street and turned right, it had already dulled to a manageable throb. He was doubly relieved, because he knew that it was likely he'd get through another couple of hours at least before having to endure another spell. The meeting would be over by then and he would hopefully be back at the hotel where he was registered as Robert Dresslyn.

Driving north on York Avenue, Levdroko continued past the busy intersection of Colfax Avenue and turned onto 17th Avenue, which finally led him to Denver's sprawling City Park. He pulled into one of the parking lots and stayed inside the Mercedes long enough to withdraw a small kit bag from his glove compartment. The individually filled syringes of medication were clearly marked as insulin injectors, but Levdroko wasn't diabetic. The clear liquid he quickly injected into his system was a morphine solution strong enough to blunt the residual pain but diluted to the extent that he could retain full control of his faculties. Within moments of being introduced to his system, the serum was already working.

Leaving the car, Levdroko walked down a winding path that ran past a children's playground and picnic area. The three men he was to see were still at the rendezvous point: a picnic table set off by itself beneath an old sycamore tree. In an effort to look inconspicuous, the men had set out a Monopoly game and were going through the motions of playing for the benefit of anyone who might be watching them.

"I see no one's using the cannon," Levdroko said, giving his coded salutation to the men as he wandered to their table. "Mind if I play?"

"Not at all," Buck Howser said. "Have a seat."

Levdroko nodded to the other two men—Wild Bill Greason and General Tom Christie. No names were mentioned, however, and no mention was made of Levdroko being late. The board was cleared and the men went through the motions of starting another game. Paper money was passed out, dice were shaken, pieces were moved and property cards were purchased, but the men's conversation had nothing to do with Monopoly. Instead they discussed the next phase of operations that the three generals planned to instigate in conjunction with the KGB.

The black-market peddling of outmoded weapons from the arsenals of DTI and Mountland Computer Enterprises was a lucrative sideline for Howser and Greason, lining their pockets with multimillion-dollar under-the-table profits every year. But both men had grander plans, plans that had led them to bring Christie and his Ryco/Kent salvaging firm into the fold.

On behalf of Ryco/Kent, General Christie had spent the better part of the past thirteen months lobbying intensely with officials both at the Department of Energy and the Nuclear Regulatory Agency. The work had finally paid off. His company had recently received a forty-three-million-dollar contract to oversee the disposal of waste materials associated with the development of nuclear weapons in a nine-state area stretching from the Upper Rockies down through the high-tech corridor in New Mexico. Among those wastes were nuclear fuel rods and defective plutonium pellets, both of which, under the right circumstances and with the right equipment, could be remanufactured into the necessary components to arm nuclear warheads.

And it was in nuclear warheads that the three generals felt the real money was to be made. Using the KGB as their distribution arm, they figured they could do a healthy business with the same Third World countries that already armed themselves with the weapons, DTI and Mountland dumped on the market. And if one of the countries in question ended up blowing itself or an enemy to oblivion, well, the men reasoned, there would be fewer lowlifes to choke the planet's resources. Levdroko, of course, fit into the equation because of his KGB affiliation and his recent exploits in New Mexico. But he was also the most knowledgeable Soviet agent when it came to the nuclear arms situation throughout the world, especially in terms of the countries who longed to join the military heavyweights but lacked the means to legitimately acquire the necessary technology.

There was little disagreement among the men as they talked over their plan and hammered out details. Following the DTI-Mountland merger, a spin-off company would join with Ryco/Kent's nuclear waste management subsidiary. The new company would falsify records and juggle inventories to account for the missing plutonium that would end up in the black-market warheads. The KGB would lend its assistance and remain the international connection between buyer and seller, thereby controlling who would receive how much nuclear power and at what time. What the Soviets sought, in a nutshell, was a way of literally calling the shots in the battle for domination of the Third World.

In sight of such volatile plans, it seemed almost petty for the men to be concerning themselves with the fate of a young amateur filmmaker, but each felt it was a matter that required the utmost priority.

"I talked to our man inside the sheriff's department," Howser explained as he moved his playing piece around the Monopoly board. "Since the woman left Salida it's like she vanished into thin air. No trace."

"And her 'escorts'?" Christie asked.

"He thought he might have spotted them out in the hills near the avalanche site," Howser said, "but it turned out to be a false alarm."

"Well," Greason said, "that girl didn't just vanish. She has to be somewhere, and the longer she's out of our sight, the more time she'll have to throw a monkey wrench in our plans.''

''You've had your chance at her,'' Levdroko said calmly. ''I think I'll have a go, if you don't mind.''

''Suit yourself,'' Howser replied. ''You know something we don't?''

''Probably not,'' Levdroko said. ''I mean, I assume you do know that there's a funeral for her uncle tomorrow.''

''Yes, and ... ?''

''And I think she'll have to be there,'' Levdroko said. ''Along with her entourage. All the sitting ducks gathered in the same pond.''

12

After his stop at Rayford's Creek Savings, Deputy Bedson had driven another two miles down the access road to the county sheriff's department, where he'd spent the next five hours. Fortunately there was a library across the street from the parking lot, and Lyons had been able to maintain his surveillance between glances at magazines pulled from the window racks.

At sunset, however, the library closed and Lyons was forced to retreat to his car, parked along a tree-lined street half a block from the sheriff's department. While he sat behind the wheel, Lyons opened a newspaper for cover and used his communicator to make contact with Blancanales. Pol reported that Lao Ti was in Denver and that the film taken from the dead prospector's camera had revealed shots of a green pickup. Although Kurtzman was doing computer scans in hopes of pinpointing the truck's owners, without a license plate it would be difficult, if not impossible. There were also discreet checks being made with local authorities to discern if the tattoo on the truck driver's arm could help narrow the search. Beyond that, plans were presently in the making for maintaining necessary security at Bones Callahan's funeral the next day.

"Well, I'll catch up with you sooner or later," Lyons grumbled. "I want to wait out Bedson and see if he goes anywhere after work."

"Which reminds me," Blancanales told him, "Kurtzman did a deep trace on that bank down the block from you. It was Bedson's payroll check that he cashed."

"Shit," Lyons cursed, almost ripping the newspaper in his frustration. "Did Bear get a balance on him?"

"Yeah. If he's getting paid by anyone else, he's being smart about hiding it."

"Figures."

"Well, hang tight, Ironman. Something's gotta give."

"Right," Lyons said cynically. "And I got a feeling it's gonna be my stomach unless I get something to eat."

"Try the headrest," Blancanales advised. "High in fiber."

There was a McDonald's farther down the block, and after getting off the communicator with Blancanales, Lyons pulled around, using the drive-through so he could maintain his surveillance. He'd just put in an order for a couple of quarter-pounders with cheese when he glanced down the street and saw Bedson leaving the sheriff's building and heading for his Samurai.

"This just isn't my day," Lyons muttered under his breath as he jerked on the steering wheel and weaved out of the line of customers waiting for take-out orders. Stomach growling, he followed Bedson onto the eastbound Midland Expressway. At the outskirts of the city, Bedson left the freeway for Garden Drive and Lyons tailed as closely as he could as the road wound its way through the majestically eerie rock formations comprising the Garden of the Gods, a 940-acre site beloved by photographers and sightseers alike.

Although the park was closed for the night, there were numerous stretches along the road where it was possible for one to trespass onto the grounds with minimal difficulty. Bedson parked his Samurai on the shoulder near one such area, forcing Lyons to drive past rather than risk blowing his cover. Fortunately there was a bend just eighty yards down the road, and although it meant Lyons had to scale a ten-foot-high facing of blasted sandstone to enter the park, he was adept enough at rock-climbing to clear the obstruction in short time.

Reaching the top of the formation, he flattened himself and crawled along the rock to a vantage point from which he could look into the park. It was a clear night, and in the moonlight he was able to pick out Bedson less than fifty yards away, skulking along a narrow trail leading to the monstrous slabs of Gateway Rocks.

As stealthily as possible, Lyons slid down from the rock he was on and sprinted toward the trail, knowing there was a risk in letting the other man out of his sight again, for however few seconds. It was a gamble he lost, because when Lyons emerged on the path and cleared the next rise, the way before him was clear. With the path surrounded by tall grass and scattered shrubs, there were any number of places Bedson could have gone.

Berating himself, Lyons reached inside his vest, pulling out his .45. He stayed put momentarily, straining all senses in hopes that Bedson would somehow betray his position. He could detect the drone of traffic off on the expressway and the closer hum of tires rounding the bend behind him. The night was also alive with the sounds of wildlife, from the chirping of crickets to the mournful cry of an owl in the nearby pines. But there were no telltale footsteps, no crackling of dry twigs being trampled underfoot.

Lyons considered backtracking to the road in hopes of picking up the surveillance once Bedson returned to his car, but he just as quickly dismissed the notion. More than likely, Bedson was here for a clandestine rendezvous—the opportunity Lyons had spent all day waiting for. It just didn't make sense for him to walk away.

Lyons quickly calculated that if he could get to one of the Gateway Rocks unnoticed and climb high enough, he'd have a clear, panoramic view of the surrounding parkland, and with any luck he'd be able to spot Bedson and whoever the deputy was meeting with.

Rather than showing himself along the main path, Lyons diverted his course, relying on a cushion of dead pine needles to soften his steps. He used the cover of trees to make his approach to the rocks, which thrust upward at steep angles like crude building blocks left behind by a giant. Lyons holstered his Colt as he inspected the facing, which was even more precipitous than the one he'd just cleared. As popular with rock climbers as with photographers, the sandstone formations were pitted and worn in spots from countless ascents, and Lyons had no trouble finding good hand and toeholds as he dragged his 190-pound frame up the steepest of the vertical shafts. Every few yards he paused, glancing over his shoulder in hopes of spotting the deputy.

Twenty feet up, the rock levelled off on one side, extending outward like an escarpment over a deep gorge carved out of the valley. Before climbing higher, Lyons decided to follow the formation to its clifflike edge and see if Bedson had possibly taken a pathway down into the gorge. As he approached the precipice, Lyons heard a noise off to his right and instinctively sprang to one side, reaching for his gun. He heard the dull crack of muffled gunfire as a bullet smacked off the rock just behind him, stinging him with shrapnel.

An unexpected dip in the rock's surface brought Lyons down with a turned ankle, sending jolts of pain ripping up his leg. Even as he was landing, his would-be assailant was scrambling across the ledge toward him. Before Lyons could come out with his .45, Bedson was standing over him with his own gun pressed against Lyon's skull.

"Move and you're a dead man," Bedson warned.

Although he looked still, Lyons cautiously tensed his muscles, ignoring the pain in favor of the more pressing concern of survival. "Geez," he complained, looking away from Bedson in hopes he wouldn't be recognized in the dim light, "can't a guy go hiking without being robbed these days?"

"You weren't hiking, shitface," Bedson hissed. "You were following me. Why?"

"I wasn't following you, man. Hey, there are plenty of rocks around here. You want this one to yourself, fine, I'll move—"

The deputy dropped to a half crouch to get a better look at Lyons and recognized him immediately. "You—"

Lyons lashed out suddenly like an uncoiled spring, throwing his head back and leaning away from Bedson's gun at the same time he swung out his legs. Bedson fired wildly as Lyons's kick sent him staggering backward.

Not wanting to lose any time going for his gun, Lyons shifted his weight and pushed off his good ankle, tackling the deputy before he could draw a clear aim. He grabbed Bedson's gun hand as they grappled and slammed it repeatedly until the weapon clattered away from them.

Although the men were roughly the same weight, Bedson was taller and he used that height difference for what little advantage it gave him, using his arms like pistons to shove Lyons away from him. Lyons had an edge on strength, however, and the bald man wasn't able to shake the Ironman's tenacious hold. Together they rolled across the hard rock, moving precariously close to the cliff's edge. Although they both grimaced loudly as they strained to overpower each other, neither spoke. At one point Lyons caught an elbow in the mouth and felt blood streak down his chin from a split lip. He countered with a knee thrust that Bedson took in the ribs, forcing him to momentarily loosen his grip.

Lyons exhaled and expended all his strength, managing to break free. It was a risky move, however, because as he recoiled from Bedson, both his legs slid over the edge of the precipice and gravity threatened to pull him down the thirty-foot drop. He had to forget about the deputy and concentrate totally on pulling himself back up. It was the break Bedson had been waiting for and he rushed forward, determined to finish Lyons off.

Up to this point, Lyons had been forced to rely on basic street-fighting tactics, but with some distance between himself and his foe, he saw a chance to exhibit some of his karate expertise. He rolled fully back onto solid ground, pivoting his weight in such a way that his legs shot upward, catching Bedson by surprise. The deputy fell headlong toward Lyons, who then bent his legs at the knees, in effect making himself a human trampoline. When he arched his back and straightened his knees again while rolling backward, Lyons managed to propel the other man over the precipice. Bedson let out a gasp of shock that was suddenly and sickeningly quieted when he landed on the rocks below.

Wiping his bleeding lip as he regained his breath, Lyons peered down the cliff and saw Bedson sprawled at an unnatural angle. He'd seen enough dead men to know that the deputy's neck had been broken.

With his ankle still throbbing with pain, Lyons moved quietly away from the ledge, still wary that another adversary might be lying in wait for him nearby. He pulled out his .45 and scanned the darkness around him. Something caught his attention, lying just beyond the shadows where the other half of the rock jutted skyward. On closer inspection, Lyons discovered that it was a plain brown grocery bag. Inside were thin stacks of twenty-dollar bills, more than ten thousand dollars worth.

"So this is where you did your other banking," Lyons murmured. "I think you just lost your interest."

13

There are likely few places in the world that can rival Colorado for the kind of scenic wonder all-American families look for when taking an idle Sunday drive. Endless back roads snake out into majestic mountain country throughout the state, and even those living close to the congested Denver-to-Colorado Springs corridor can put the city far behind them in a few minutes.

Route 59, however, was another matter.

Once a major thoroughfare, this east-west two-lane strip, running from Oreville to the sparsely populated lowlands of Elbert County, saw a different type of Sunday traveler. Beginning at shortly before dawn, the first rumbling drones of motorcycles would thunder through the hills, and by noon the din would be incessant. Caravan after caravan of two-wheelers would make their weekly pilgrimage to Aspen Meadows, a former hunting lodge now doing business as a liquor store, dispensing as much liquid refreshment on Sunday afternoons as some major league ballparks.

Some of the motorcycles were driven by middle-aged retirees and weekend hobbyists cultivating some part-time fascination with the feeling of rugged individualism that came with riding loud in the open air. They parked their bulky, factory-issue road machines, with their gleaming metallic saddlebags and bug-splattered windshields, on the east side of the lodge. The bikes were tightly packed, like an encircled wagon train defending itself against attack by renegade forces. In this case, rather than rebellious Indian tribes, the renegades in question were the members of more than three hundred different motorcycle clubs and gangs living within a five-state radius of Colorado. Remarkably—given the temperaments of the riders, the amounts of alcohol consumed and the natural intramural rivalries between gangs—there was little violence during these tribal gatherings and even fewer road fatalities before and after the store opened its doors.

It was shortly after one-thirty when Randall Howser showed up, still hung over from the fifth of Wild Turkey he'd downed the previous day after being evicted by his father. It had been an ugly time. Shacking up with Erica at her Larkspur apartment, he'd tried drowning his anger in bourbon and cocaine, and Erica had provided her share of distraction, tolerating his coarse lovemaking and even playing along with it to an extent. But his rage at his father couldn't be so easily forgotten, and in time it had seized hold of him and he'd lashed out at Erica, striking her hard across the face with the back of his hand. Bleeding from a cut lip, the woman had retaliated in self-defense, kicking him in the groin before grabbing his bowie knife and threatening to use it in the most painful way imaginable if he so much as touched her again.

By then, however, Randall was teetering on the edge of losing consciousness and the painful ache between his legs had left him nauseous. He remembered staggering into the bathroom and kneeling before the toilet to purge himself, but beyond that there was a nine-hour gap of total blackness. He'd awakened alone in the apartment, face against the cold tiles of the bathroom door, dried vomit caked to the side of his face. Erica was nowhere to be found, not having left so much as a note. After a shower and a cup of instant coffee, he'd ridden his bike to the Happy Trails Hotel, bloodshot eyes shielded by dark sunglasses, only to be told it was her day off. And so he'd continued eastbound to the Meadows, seeking the consolation of his own kind.

The store was crowded and it took him nearly fifteen minutes to buy lunch, a six-pack of Rainer's Ale, four strips of beef jerky and two Dolly Madison fruit pies. Devouring the food between sips of ale, Randall meandered through the throng of fellow bikers, feeling nourished not only by the food and drink but also by the familiar, pungent aroma given off by the assembled multitude. Marijuana blended with the smoke from cigarettes, and there was a pervasive mingling of body odors.

But Randall was thinking of only one thing now—revenge.

The old man had showed him up for the last time, Randall had decided. He was going to get back . . . for years of abuse. It was a large score to settle, and he wanted to make sure that the retribution made its greatest impact. It wouldn't do to just kill his father—that would be too easy. No, he wanted to hurt him, to make him feel some of the humiliation Randall had endured since the death of his brother all those years ago. That wouldn't be easy. Buck Howser was a hardened man.

But Randall knew a way. He only needed some help to carry out the plan.

As expected, he found the Heathens in their usual spot, under the shade cast by a stand of aspens just off the edge of the parking lot. There were fourteen of the bikers, sporting the gang's colors and tattoos, leaning against their bikes, swilling bear and tossing empties in a single heap at the base of the closest tree.

"Yo, Also-Rand," the group's leader sniggered as Randall joined them.

Nicknamed Syracuse for his hometown, the head Heathen was a thin man in his mid-twenties, sporting a broad, raised scar across his face where he'd been gashed by a broken beer bottle during a bar brawl four years ago. He had a week's worth of beard and a gold star embedded in one of his front teeth. He was flanked by the gang's enforcers, a monolithic pair who were living proof that man most likely descended from the ape.

"Let's talk, Syracuse," Randall told the other man, ignoring the bodyguards.

"About what?" Syracuse wondered. "Same old conversation? You want to use the old man's money to buy yourself some colors?"

Randall calmly shook his head. "Not even close."

"Oh?" Syracuse looked at the other gang members and smirked. "This could get interesting. Let's have it."

"Not here," Randall said. He gestured off to his right, where a toppled lodgepole pine was slowly disintegrating into the earth. "Just you, Danny and José."

Syracuse glanced over at the men in question, then back at Randall. "What gives, huh?"

"Let's talk and you'll find out," Randall bartered. He chewed down his last beef jerky and crumpled the wrapper in his fist before dropping it to the ground at Syracuse's feet.

Intrigued by Randall's self-confidence, Syracuse motioned for his bodyguards to stay put and ventured away from his prized Harley, followed by Danny and José. Randall led them over to the felled pine. Another gang was idling a few yards away, but in deference to the Heathens reputation as one of the more violent outfits in the state, they cleared out to give them more room.

"Okay, Also-Rand," Syracuse said when the four men were alone. "What's on your mind?"

"I want in," Randall said matter-of-factly. "And I already did my initiation."

"That so?"

"That's right." Randall looked over at Danny, a man of medium build with a thick brown mustache and cold gray eyes. "Tell him, Danny."

"He's right, Syracuse. He iced some guy up north a couple days ago. Did a real pro job. Me and José helped bury him."

"Who?" Syracuse wanted to know.

"Businessman," Randall explained. "But that doesn't matter. You bring me in, I've got a way to put the Heathens into some choice goods."

"Like what?"

Randall paused to light a cigarette and open another can of Rainer's, smiling thinly. He could tell that he already had Syracuse on the hook. Now to play him a little.

"My old man's been putting together a secret installation out in the hills around Manitou Springs," he explained casually. "Kind of a glorified warehouse."

"For what?" Syracuse asked.

"Weapons," Randall said. "Old issues and obsolete inventory, mostly. He's got a sweetheart deal with some firm that's supposed to recycle all these guns and shit. What they do is just fudge the paperwork and throw in some scrap metal to pass for the stuff they take out to the hills."

"And what do they do with it out there?"

"Peddle it on the black market," Randall said. "Third World, drug runners, anybody who can come up with the cash, basically. It's been a nice little sideline, but now he's gearing up to go big-time."

Syracuse ran a finger along his scar, then reached behind his ear for a toothpick. Placing it between his teeth, he said, "Maybe I'm missing something, but what's this got to do with us?"

"I think you know," Randall said. "You let me in, I help us stage a raid on the installation. We do it right, it's a two, maybe three million dollar job."

Randall smiled around his toothpick. "I like those kind of numbers. Tell me more."

"First things first," Randall said. "Am I in?"

Syracuse shrugged. "Have to put it to a vote, but probably. What else?"

"Quit calling me Also-Rand."

14

Aaron Kurtzman had been crippled below the waist since taking a bullet to the spine during a failed siege of the Stony Man compound a number of years ago. While lesser men might have given up in the face of such a tragedy, Kurtzman had risen to the challenge of his handicap, refusing to surrender either his enthusiasm or resourcefulness in his chosen field. His ongoing dedication kept him on the cutting edge of technology, and the breadth of his computer expertise was such that he was constantly outwitting the programmers of various law enforcement agencies both at home and abroad.

If the Bear felt that a mission required tapping into confidential files, access was inevitable, no matter how sophisticated that particular data bank's security system was. In several cases, he was on retainer for those same agencies, providing them with helpful hints as to ways they could better protect themselves against infiltration from the outside.

Huddled over consoles in the Farm's first-floor computer room, Kurtzman's fingers danced back and forth between three separate keyboards as his eyes tracked the pulsing glow of data turning up on the bank of monitors in front of him. It was a dizzying performance, almost as if he was a grandmaster chessman playing several games simultaneously. Absorbed as he was in his work, Kurtzman didn't notice Hal Brognola enter the room behind him. It was only when he finished a complicated series of commands and leaned back for a moment's respite that he acknowledged the other man's presence.

"Any progress?" Brognola asked.

"Nothing significant," Bear confessed. "This genetic imprinting's a new field, so I'm sort of making up a network as I go along."

"Sounds like just the kind of project you like to sink your mainframe into," Brognola said.

"Yep," Bear admitted.

Two separate teams of forensic pathologists had been working overtime trying to glean as many clues as possible from the few strands of hair and the blood sample that had been flown in from Rayford's Creek. Kurtzman's contribution had been to set up the computer link between the two laboratories, which were located more than four hundred and fifty miles apart. As data came in from either lab, Kurtzman entered it into a third work file, which he referred to while logging additional programs. It was his hope that between the three of them, they would speed up the time it would normally take to crack the genetic code and uncover the identity of the deceased.

"I know it's a foolish question," Brognola said, "but is there any chance you can free up a little time and get one of the computers going on that other project?''

"I'm way ahead of you, Chief."

Kurtzman wheeled himself away from the main grid of computer terminals and led Brognola across the room to the far wall, where a backup computer system was buzzing with a life of its own.

"Got this baby pretty much on autopilot," Bear boasted, patting the mainframe. "I'm running checks on all available shipping lanes, air cargo flights, train routes—any transportation records that might turn up the way these weapons are getting to the Third World."

"You mean you can do all that without having to baby-sit some keyboard?''

"That's right," Kurtzman said. "Computers are just like people. If you get the language down pat and learn how to talk to them the right way, they'll bend over backward to do you a favor."

Brognola shook his head with a look of amazement. "You're one of a kind, Bear. I don't know where we'd be without you."

"You'd need the Empire State Building filled with three-by-five cards and a couple of thousand people to shuffle them into order...for starters," Kurtzman said with a grin.

Brognola returned the smile. "Why do I get the feeling you're bucking for a raise here?"

"Must be psychic, boss."

"Yeah, right," Brognola said. "Tell you what, though. You come up with a major breakthrough on either front in the next twelve hours, I'll give you first dibs on those Redskins tickets I've got lined up through the Bureau."

"Now you're talking," Kurtzman said, rubbing his palms together. He glanced up at the wall clock. It was already after six. He'd had a vague notion of getting to bed before midnight, but that thought quickly vanished from his mind. He told Brognola, "When you go back upstairs, tell 'em to get a fresh pot of coffee brewing. It's going to be one hell of a night!"

"That's the spirit." Brognola gave his associate a good-natured nudge on the shoulder. "And, just to make it interesting, if you hit pay dirt on both fronts, I'll get the Farm to underwrite your walking program. What do you say?"

Kurtzman's face turned red with embarrassment and he glanced up at Brognola. "How'd you know about that?"

Brognola smiled. "That's not important. How's it coming along?"

They were referring to a confidential project Kurtzman was undertaking during what little free time he mustered between official Stony Man business. His plan was to implement computers in an attempt to plot out some kind of device that would allow the brain to bypass the injured segment of his spine and transmit commands to his lower extremities to enable him to walk again. There had been countless ventures along the same lines instigated by the medical profession over the years. Kurtzman was compiling all the cumulative data and trying to streamline the workings, hoping to one day strike upon an apparatus that would meet the threefold need of lightweight portability, low-cost maintenance and rugged durability. John Kissinger, the Farm's armorer, had agreed to assemble any noncomputerized components and a pair of unsuccessful prototypes had already been put together and tested. In each case the contraptions had been too uncomfortable to wear and too sporadic in overall effectiveness. At best they only produced a series of uncoordinated twitches, which were miraculous breakthroughs in their own right, but far from the final product Kurtzman envisioned as being a vital tool in his rehabilitation and that of others who shared similar afflictions.

"That's still in the pipe-dream phase," Bear conceded. "Even if I could devote all my time to it, there's still a great deal of work left to be done."

"You haven't had a leave of absence since that bullet put you in the hospital five years ago, Aaron," Brognola told him. "You're overdue for a break. Maybe now's the time."

"Thanks, but there's so much to catch up on here that I—"

"If I have to, I'll make it an order," Brognola said.

Kurtzman shook his head. "Look, let's get through these couple things, then I'll think about it, okay?"

"Let's get through this, then you'll *do* it."

Bear couldn't help but grin. "You sure know how to drive a hard bargain."

Brognola grinned back at him. "Spare me the flattery and get back to work."

"Aye, aye, sir."

15

To the majority of those gathered at Heaven's Vista Cemetery in the hills near Cripple Creek, the graveside services for Bones Callahan were simply the last rites being delivered to a decent man who had touched their lives and was now gone. However, a closer look would have revealed that the gathering had more to do with the preservation of life than the rituals of death.

For starters, of the six pallbearers who had lifted the coffin from the hearse to the burial site, two were strangers to everyone else at the gathering. Lyons and Grimaldi had passed themselves off as close friends who knew Bones before he moved to Colorado. Wearing dark glasses, they stood near the deep hole in the ground that would become Bones Callahan's final resting place, watching the crowd for any sign of someone who might have come to the ceremony with the intention of harming Pamela. They could see John Kissinger roaming the periphery of the cemetery, wearing a suit and acting the part of liaison for the funeral home handling the service. Closer by, Pol Blancanales and Gadgets Schwarz flanked a woman in a somber black pantsuit who was wearing a thick black

veil to help further disguise the fact that she wasn't
Pamela Callahan at all, but rather Lao Ti. Like the
other five commandos from Stony Man Farm, she had
an automatic pistol secreted in its shoulder holster. All
six of them hoped like hell there wouldn't be a need to
use the weapons in a setting where innocent bystand-
ers would likely suffer the greatest casualties in any
confrontation.

Pamela, disguised in an auburn wig and makeup
that made her look a good fifteen years older, mingled among the other mourners a few rows back from
her double. She knew it was important not to betray
the ruse Able Team had engineered on her behalf, but
as she listened to the moving eulogy delivered by the
pastor of the church her uncle had attended most of
his years in Colorado, she couldn't help but weep, not
only with grief but also with pride for the man who
had been such an important part of her life.

Even as the priest was speaking of the so-called accident that had claimed Bones's life, Kissinger, on the
lookout for those responsible for the man's murder,
noticed a suspicious-looking couple lingering in the
parking lot thirty yards away from the burial grounds.
They were standing near the rear of a car whose trunk
hood had been raised more than six minutes ago. Pe-
riodically the couple would glance toward the grave
site, but they stayed put, exchanging whispers.

Kissinger waited until he had the attention of the
other men, then gestured at the parking lot before
drawing in a deep breath and going to confront the
couple. He nonchalantly unbuttoned his coat to give

him freer access to his automatic. If there was to be trouble, he hoped he'd be able to keep it away from the crowd. The fact that he was wearing a Kevlar-mesh vest was of some small comfort, but he knew that if he was marching into the midst of professional killers, they wouldn't be stupid enough to waste ammunition on his chest. They'd try to drill him between the eyes.

As he drew closer, the man dropped from view behind the trunk hood and Kissinger tensed, bracing himself for the worst.

"Anything I can help you folks with?" he called out quietly.

"No thank you," the woman said. She was in her late forties, thick-framed with pudgy features. Her eyes were visibly red and she dabbed at them with a handkerchief as she spoke. "We're just waiting for the service to end. Our son's buried next to the man they're burying now."

As he rounded the car, Kissinger saw that the man was tending to a large floral bouquet set in the trunk. He glanced up at Kissinger, sorrow in his eyes, as well. "Lost him to a drunk driver," he said, his voice cracking. "Just out of high school. . . ."

Moved as he was by their apparent sincerity, Kissinger nonetheless maintained his guard, watching for any sign that the couple's story was only a front. He discreetly glanced into the trunk and noted the couple's clothes, checking for any indication of concealed weapons. Once he was satisfied that they were on the level, he smiled politely and told them, "My condolences to you both. We should be finished here shortly."

"Fine," the woman said. "We don't mind waiting."

Kissinger turned and headed back to the graveside ceremony. He missed seeing the man lean down toward the trunk, cocking his head so he could speak into a small condenser microphone planted on the underside of the hood.

"WELL, THAT SURE WENT smoothly enough," Schwarz said as he loosened his tie.

He was in the back seat of a black limousine inching down the steep mountain road linking Heaven's Vista Cemetery with the outside world. Lao Ti sat beside him, still disguised as Pamela Callahan, and Blancanales was up front driving, carefully negotiating the sharp turns.

"Too smoothly, if you ask me," Blancanales said as he wrestled with the steering wheel.

"I knew you were going to say that," Schwarz said. "And you're right. It was just too ripe an opportunity for them to have passed up."

"Well," Lao Ti suggested, "why look a gift horse in the mouth? There could be any number of explanations for them not making a hit back there."

"I know that," Blancanales admitted. "But it just doesn't add up. We have to go on the premise that they want to shut Pamela up the same way they did Bones...it's the only explanation that washes for me.

And given the fact that she disappeared on them, this was their best chance.''

"True," Lao Ti said. The wig and veil were both bothering her, but she wasn't about to take them off. Although she had voiced doubts that their charade had served any purpose, she knew better than to drop her guard and call off the plan until it had run its full course. If the enemy was still lurking out there somewhere, the game wasn't over yet. They still had to return to the church where memorial services had been held, then play out the scene of moving her to a "safe house" other than the ranger's cabin where John Kissinger was now taking the real Pamela Callahan.

The past two days had been nothing like Lao Ti had expected when she'd decided to drop in on Stony Man Farm, and yet she suspected that perhaps she really had hoped to become involved in one of the Team's missions. Riding with Pol and Gadgets, .45 automatic secreted inside her coat, she could feel the kind of adrenaline rush that comes only from putting one's life on the line. For the first time since her last impromptu assignment with the group, she once again felt that incomparable feeling the warrior gets while in the thick of the battle...that feeling that no moment counts but the here and now.

"The important thing is that Pamela's still okay," Schwarz said. "Mission accomplished on that front."

"Now we just have to figure out our next move," Blancanales said.

As the three of them discussed strategy, Lao Ti stared out the window, taking in the breathtaking scenery. Just beyond the guardrail, there was a sharp drop-off into a deep, pine-strewn ravine, and off in the distance a series of mountain ranges that stretched for miles before melding into the distant horizon. Several hawks could be seen floating in lazy circles above the cavity, riding air currents as their shadows roved across the greenery below. Although she was admiring the view, Lao's senses were still on alert. When she spotted a quick glint of sunlight reflecting off something down in the ravine, the woman instantly focused her full attention on it. Her eyes widened with sudden horror as she realized the source of the glint was a rifle scope.

"Sniper at nine o'clock!" she cried out.

Before anyone could react, however, a shot slammed into the front windshield. The glass was bullet-proof, but the impact of the slug created a spiderweb of cracks that obscured Pol's view. As if that weren't enough of a hindrance, a second shot, following close on the heels of the first, took out the limo's right front wheel.

"Damn!" Blancanales cursed as he fought the steering wheel and pumped the foot brake. It was a losing battle, as the car was already out of control. Halfway down the steep incline, the limo went into a full spin, crashing through the thick guardrail and over the side of the mountain.

Both Schwarz and Blancanales, their reflexes honed by years of training, had the presence of mind to go limp as they felt themselves hurtling down the treacherous incline of the cliff. Lao Ti also knew better than to tighten her body, and the cry she let out was less one of fear than of expelling as much tension as possible from her system.

Fortunately, all three were wearing seat belts, and although the limo rolled over twice before landing on its side in a loamy ditch, none of its passengers were thrown from their seats. Still, it had been a jarringly traumatic crash, and nobody moved for several seconds after the limo had come to a complete halt, wedged between a pair of gargantuan boulders.

As Schwarz came to, he felt a trickle of blood running down his forehead. He'd bruised his shoulder, as well, and he was pinned under the weight of Lao Ti, who was dazed, clinging to the barest thread of consciousness. Pol groaned up in front, feeling a sharp pain in his chest and ribs where he'd struck the steering wheel, which had collapsed at a slight angle, making it hard for him to get at the keys. Although the engine had stalled, he was anxious to turn off the ignition, as he smelled a pungent odor.

"Gas," he muttered, tugging himself out of his seat belt. "Let's get out of here!"

With the limo tipped on its side, maneuvering was difficult, and the fact that the driver's door had been crushed to the point where it could not be opened hindered Blancanales's race against time. He finally crawled over the back of his seat, trying to blot out the searing pain in his ribs as he helped Schwarz drag Lao Ti up and out of the limo through the back door.

Within seconds of their escape there was a small explosion in the engine compartment. The two men dragged Lao Ti as quickly as possible across the craggy terrain, so that when the gas tank ignited seconds later, they were clear of the spray of metallic shrapnel that showered the rocks around them.

A little more than twenty yards away, the sedan carrying Lyons and Grimaldi lay in a similarly twisted heap. It had also been the victim of snipers' bullets. Both men had survived the crash, and Gadgets took heart in the sight of them scrambling from the wreckage toward the nearest boulders.

"You all in one piece?" Lyons shouted back at Schwarz.

"I think so," Schwarz replied.

By now Lao Ti was conscious, although her face was already beginning to swell from where she'd collided with Gadgets's shoulder during the crash. She was just rising to her feet and reaching for her automatic when another rifle shot sounded and she took the slug in the chest, right below her heart. The impact of the shot alone was enough to knock her off balance, and she spun awkwardly before landing facedown in the dirt.

"Pamela!" Schwarz cried out, crouching at the woman's side and lightly nudging her shoulder. Lao Ti wasn't moving, however.

"Bastards!" Blancanales howled, helping Schwarz drag the woman to cover as a second shot slammed into the ground near their feet.

As near as Blancanales could figure, they'd been caught in a cross fire between two different riflemen. By tracing the trajectory of one of the shots, he was able to make out the shadowy outline of a sniper crouched behind a cluster of bushes up next to the shattered guardrail the two cars had crashed through. Quickly switching his M-1911A to its potent 3-shot mode, Pol took a two-handed firing stance and unleashed three separate 3-shot bursts. The slugs chewed through the underbrush, seeking out their target, and there was a howl of agony as the sniper spun clear of his cover, spewing blood from a chest wound. He'd already dropped his weapon, and when Schwarz drilled him with another two shots, the gunman died a quick and brutal death.

"One down," Blancanales musęd bitterly, breaking from cover and scrambling across the rock formations. There were at least two other snipers positioned elsewhere in the ravine, and after taking only a few steps toward Lyons and Grimaldi he was forced to dive to the ground as bullets peppered the rock formations around him.

"Could use a little backup, guys," he muttered under his breath.

As if in answer to Pol's prayer, Grimaldi took aim over the crumpled front end of the backup car and squeezed off a spray of eight single shots in the general vicinity of another of the snipers. There came a muffled cry deep within the brush, followed by a snapping of twigs as the once-hidden rifleman toppled into the open, bleeding from a bullet wound that had neatly pierced his skull.

Back up on the road, other cars heading back from the funeral service had slowed down, aware of the disturbance. Lyons had already scrambled up the steep incline of the ravine and he shouted at the onlookers, "Go on, get the hell out of here! Get out of here!"

The couple who had been spying on the funeral service had stopped their car near the break in the railing. The woman, who was riding in the passenger seat, had managed to train her binoculars on Lao Ti just before she'd taken the hit. As she slipped the glasses beneath her seat, she turned to the man beside her. "Do like he says. At least they got the woman."

Lyons wasn't about to waste any more time than necessary directing traffic. He blasted away at one of the snipers posted clear across the ravine, then bounded downhill to come to the assistance of his colleague. His labored breathing was drowned out by the rattle of more gunfire and he was forced to dive headlong through a thicket to avoid being perforated by sniper fire coming from a point halfway down the ravine. One bullet skimmed off his shoulder, drawing blood through the material of his shirt.

But the snipers had already missed their best chance of neutralizing Able Team. When the men all emerged intact from the mangled wreckage of the two automobiles, it had only been a matter of time before their unsurpassed experience turned the odds in their favor. In a little less than six minutes, the shoot-out was over and three riflemen lay dead in the ravine. Their accomplices had apparently hightailed it to their waiting vehicles.

As the others went to check on the assailants and make sure there weren't more lurking in the brush,

Blancanales climbed back over to where Lao Ti had fallen earlier.

"Tough break, lady," he said, placing a hand on the woman's shoulder.

"I'll say," Lao Ti whispered, opening one eye and winking at Blancanales. "But things would have been even tougher if I hadn't been wearing a vest."

Although Lao Ti had taken a direct hit to the chest, the slug had flattened against a layer of Kevlar rather than flesh and bone. She had been stunned by the force of the bullet, but was otherwise unscathed.

"Just stay put in case they've got someone watching," Blancanales told her. "We want them to think they at least got Pamela out of the picture."

Schwarz, meanwhile, had gone over to the closest of the fallen assailants and was frisking him for clues as to his identity and the identity of whoever had contracted him to make the hit. Knowing that the killer was undoubtedly a professional, Gadgets held little hope that his search would reveal anything. To his surprise, however, he found a telltale packet of matches in the man's pants pocket.

"The Handlebar, San Francisco," he muttered to Lyons, who had climbed over to join him.

"That's a KGB drop-point, isn't it?" Lyons said.

Schwarz nodded. "Sure as hell is. And I can think of one man who ties neatly into Frisco and the KGB and whatever the hell's going on here in Colorado."

Lyons nodded knowingly. "Levdroko," he said.

16

Six miles north of Rayford's Creek was a thirteen-hundred-acre parcel of private land set squarely in the heart of unruly mountain country. Too treacherous for development or road construction, the land had been left largely untouched over the years. It showed only a few telltale scars from when, like the rest of Colorado, the area had been besieged by ore-seeking miners who bored deep into its bowels in search of the next mother lode. Of all the land mined throughout the state, however, this parcel had proved the least productive. For a fifty-year period between World War I and the height of U.S. involvement in Southeast Asia, the land had fallen under the control of the Park Service and become the Lost Mines Wildlife Refuge, providing a home for numerous species displaced by housing developments in adjacent communities.

In the late sixties, however, a deal was struck whereby more than 550 acres in the center of the refuge were sold to a consortium that consisted primarily of retired Air Force generals living in nearby Colorado Springs. One of the old mining camps had been renovated into a string of rustic cabins and a huge lodge had been built. The site provided the men with a place where they could leave the world behind and indulge themselves in days of game-hunting and nights of poker-playing. Rumor had it that for a time a full-time brothel was maintained at the camp.

Over the past twenty years, however, the novelty of the camp had dwindled and most of the generals found their diversions closer to home. When Buck Howser made an offer to the consortium two years ago to buy out their interest in the property, the deal went through with few snags. Through further negotiations with the Park Service, Howser added another 345 acres to his holdings, further isolating the land tract from the outside world.

In fact, by the time they reached the security gate at the entrance to the property, Howser and Levdroko had already driven more than a half hour along a rut-choked dirt road without encountering another motorist.

"How do you get here during the winter?" Levdroko asked as he stared out at the rampant foliage surrounding the roadway.

"Chopper," Howser said, downshifting the Jeep as he made one last sharp turn and pulled up to the gate. On the other side of the barbed-wire enclosure, six massive rottweilers suddenly lurched out from the side of a small cinder-block guard station set thirty yards inside the compound. Howling with seemingly unchecked malice, the dogs scampered back and forth near the gate, eyes on the idling Jeep.

"Cheerful fellows, aren't they," Levdroko remarked. "They'd keep me out."

"If they didn't, there are two guards inside that shack, with a pair of Uzis and a LAW launcher between them," Howser said. "And that's just the tip of the iceberg."

One of the Uzi-toting guards emerged from the station booth, shouting a few commands to the dogs as he marched to the gate. The rottweilers fell silent and scampered back to the guardhouse as the man removed a key from his pocket and unlocked the gate's security lock system. There was a second's pause, then the gates parted on well-oiled rollers, creating a gap through which Howser could drive. He exchanged nods with the guard as they drove past.

It was still another mile to the old camp, and the road had been deliberately laid out in such a way as to avoid quick access. In several places they dipped sharply along the pitched slope of a long-running ditch, and at another point they were forced to a crawl as Howser inched the Jeep across a rock-strewn creek.

"If it's hard for us when we know where we're going," Howser explained, "it's going to be that much more difficult for someone who's never been here before."

Levdroko nodded, impressed. He said nothing, however, as the torturous ride had finally taken its toll and his jaws were clenched in an effort to fight back a sudden surge of pain inside his skull. He drew in a deep breath through his nose and let it out slowly through his mouth, trying to shift his focus away from the raging agony. Beads of sweat began to form above his upper lip. Inside his coat was the small case with a syringe that could bring him partial relief, but he knew there was no way he would betray either his condition or his dependence on the drug. Instead he continued to breathe, slowly in and slowly out, until finally they cleared one last rise and rolled down a steep drive to the camp.

At first glance the string of seven small cabins and the old timber lodge could have easily been mistaken for some kind of summer youth camp. However, the forty-four workers who lived out of the cramped barracks were anything but children. Hand-picked by Howser over the years, the men were all hardened warriors, most of them with military stints under their belts. They had all demonstrated a willingness to follow orders that was surpassed only by their willingness to protect the secret of their function at the camp, where they lived twenty-five days of every month.

Howser pulled to a stop in front of the lodge and killed the Jeep's engine. "I want to check on my people a minute," he told Levdroko, "then I'll take you to the mine. Hey, are you all right?"

"Fine," the Russian said. "Just a little road sick, I'm afraid."

"Sorry about that."

"No problem," Levdroko assured him. "I'll just use the rest room and then wait for you here."

Howser pointed him in the right direction, then headed off to one of the cabins, where a khaki-clad man in his early thirties could be seen through the opened doorway, talking on a shortwave radio.

Levdroko maintained his self-control until he was safely inside the rest room, then he collapsed to his knees at one of the toilets, retching violently. There were streaks of blood in his vomit, and as he struggled to his feet Levdroko wiped at his mouth with a wad of toilet paper, staining it crimson. He glanced at himself in the mirror and was disgusted with the pallid, ill-looking man who stared back at him. This was no way to live, he thought to himself as he rolled up one sleeve of his shirt and prepared the syringe. And no way to die....

The morphine solution helped blunt the pain, and after washing his face with cold water, Levdroko felt appreciably better. He passed through the main room of the lodge on his way out, taking note of the stuffed animal heads mounted on the walls—elk, deer, bear, even a moose. Quite a trophy selection, he mused darkly. Perhaps one day soon he'd be able to present the Politburo with the heads of the men from Able Team. Of course, if he failed at this mission, Levdroko knew it could well be his head that the KGB would have mounted.

Ironically, when Levdroko returned to the Jeep, it was Howser who now looked miserable. "I thought those guys you hired for the ambush were pros," he said to the Russian.

"They are," Levdroko said, feeling a sudden flash of worry. "I used them on seven other hits. Why do you ask? Did something go wrong?"

"Well," Howser told him, "the bad news is you aren't going to get any more hits out of them. They're all dead."

"What?"

"You heard me," Howser said. "The good news, though, is at least they were able to take out the girl before they bought it."

Levdroko was silent a moment. He couldn't believe it. The snipers were part of an elite force he'd put together during his San Francisco days. They were top-flight assassins and had carried out every previous mission without a hitch. And now they were dead?

"What went wrong?"

Howser explained the situation as best he knew, relying on the report from the couple who'd helped set up the ambush following Bones Callahan's funeral.

"And what about the men with her?" Levdroko queried, already suspecting the answer he was about to get.

"Looks like they all got through it," Howser said. "So that's just going to make things a little harder. We'll have to decide whether to put things on hold for a while or push up the schedules."

"I think the latter," Levdroko said.

"We'll talk about it later," Howser replied, climbing back into the Jeep. "For now, let me show you how things are going with the mine."

NEAR THE STONE GATEWAY to Hamstead Acres was a thick growth of shrubs that provided good cover for Randall and his two Heathen buddies as they waited for Buck Howser to leave the subdivision for his rendezvous with Oleg Levdroko. As soon as the general had driven past, the three men had broken from cover and slipped unseen over the stone wall, scrambling down an embankment. There was a small creek that meandered through the development, and they walked along its uneven bank as they made their way to the Howser estate.

Randall had never covered this route on foot, and he was surprised how much longer it took than by using the road. After the first half mile, he had broken into a sweat and his breathing was labored. Beside him, Danny and José seemed to be taking the hike in stride, though they were beginning to show signs of tiring.

"Shit, man, why didn't we just stick to the road?" Danny grumbled, plucking up a stone and flinging it into the surrounding brush. A startled rabbit bolted from its cover nearby and scampered up the hillside. Danny quickly reached inside the waistband of his jeans, pulling out a .22 pistol. Before he could take aim at the rabbit, however, José swerved over and brushed the gun aside as he slammed Danny into a tree.

"What do you think you're doing, you moron!" the Hispanic hissed in his friend's face. "We're down here in this gully because we don't want to be noticed. Get it? You fire that damn popgun and we're going to have the whole neighborhood down here!"

Danny stared back sourly at José, then slowly put his gun back in his pants and nodded his head. "Yeah, you're right," he said. "Dumb idea."

"Good, we agree on something," José said. "That almost makes my day."

"Come on, let's get this over with," Randall badgered them.

Falling silent, they resumed their trek. Most of the path along the creek was well worn, but in several places they had to bypass washouts or spots where trees or foliage had obscured the trail. As expected, taking this route kept them well hidden from the residents of Hamstead Acres, although a couple of times they came across groups of children playing farther up the hill.

It took over forty-five minutes for them to reach the edge of the Howser property, then another five minutes to scale the steep grade of the embankment leading up to level ground. As they cleared the rise, the three men paused to catch their breath, hiding in the cover of tall weeds.

"Great," José muttered, glancing off to his right. "Just our luck."

Thirty yards away, a middle-aged man was sitting astride a riding lawn mower, trimming the grass on his two acres of land next door to Buck Howser.

"Relax," Randall told him. "He won't be able to hear a thing over the racket that thing's making."

"Yeah, but he might see us."

Randall shook his head. "Look how big that yard is. Once he makes his next turn, he'll have his back to us for a good forty, forty-five seconds. Plenty of time.''

''If you say so.''

They waited patiently, and once the older man had rounded a corner and was moving his way in the opposite direction, they broke cover and scrambled to the Cyclone fence surrounding Howser's property. With minimal difficulty they scaled the fence and leapt down to the other side.

''See, that wasn't so hard,'' Randall said.

''True,'' Danny said, trying to hold back a grin as he glanced at José. ''Piece of cake....''

''Oh, shit,'' José said, pointing directly ahead. ''What about those?''

Buck Howser had acquired rottweilers for himself when he'd furnished attack dogs for his mountain enclave, and all four of the canines were now rushing out from near the main house, jaws slavering as they closed in on the intruders. Danny once again acted on instinct and went for his gun. This time it was Randall who intervened, though, signaling the biker to keep the gun hidden. He stepped forward and held one arm out at an angle as he shouted, ''Ten hut!''

As if on cue, all four of the dogs slowed down and, less than five yards away, sat on their haunches and stared obediently at Randall, tongues hanging halfway out their jaws as they waited for the next command. None of them so much as looked at the other two bikers.

''At ease,'' Randall called out. The dogs rose to their paws and moved in closer to the men, sniffing their pants and shoes. Danny and José both eyed the creatures warily. "Don't worry," Randall said. "I'm the one who did most of their training. We're fine."

"I hope you're right," Danny said. "They're smelling me like I'm dog food."

"Fall in!" Randall commanded as he led the others toward the main house. The dogs trotted alongside the men, now more companions than aggressors. They easily made it past the guest cottage before the neighbor had ridden his mower back into view.

Although nearly every biker in the Heathens was proficient at handling repairs on their own choppers, José was the most mechanically inclined of the group and his expertise extended beyond the components of a motorcycle. Electronics and computers were a sideline he'd mastered over the years, and when faced with the task of bypassing Buck Howser's state-of-the-art, high-tech security system, he knew he was up to the challenge. He'd brought along a small kit bag filled with precision tools, and after Randall had pinpointed the system's control center just inside the side entrance, he took out the necessary instruments to temporarily compromise the system without setting off any alarms or showing significant signs of tampering.

Danny's specialty was picking locks, and once the alarm around the side door was disabled, he put his skills to use, tickling the tumblers until they fell in line. Randall sent the dogs off, then all three men stole into the main house.

While José went to work shutting down the main console for the entire alarm system, Danny glanced around the interior, whistling with admiration at the collection of bric-a-brac and other garish furnishings that suited Howser's questionable tastes. "Sheesh," he muttered, "I haven't seen this much kitsch under one roof since I went on the Graceland tour. Hey, Randall, you got Elvis living here or something."

"Very funny," Randall drawled sarcastically as he headed down the hallway to another locked door. "Get your ass over here, Danny, and pick this one, too," he called.

"Say please," Danny taunted as he wandered over. Unlike José, he only needed a palm-size leather pouch filled with small files and picks to get his mission accomplished. The door had a quality lock, but when pitted against a quality picker, the lock always loses. In less than two minutes, Danny had the door open and the three of them descended to the basement, which had been converted into a combination command post and war room.

"Nice setup," José said as he glanced over the large chamber. There were numerous file cabinets lining one wall, and another was filled completely with a glass-covered gun rack. On display were nearly two dozen different weapons, ranging from a few antique Colt .45s to newer and more sophisticated firearms, including some of those now part of Howser's gun-smuggling scheme.

"Dig that Ingram," Danny said, eyeing the mounted submachine gun as he tapped on the glass. "How about we take it for a souvenir."

"Forget it, cheesebrain," José said. "We've gone through all this trouble so the old man won't know we've been here, you think we're gonna walk off with one of his prized popguns?"

"And anyway," Randall told him, "once we pull this job off, you're going to have more guns than you know what to do with."

On the north wall, Randall finally pinpointed what they'd broken into the house to look for. Several schematic diagrams of the mountain camp were posted on corkboard, showing the layout of the barracks and the mineworks. All guard posts were clearly indicated, and in one of the adjacent file cabinets were even more detailed documents that would prove invaluable when planning a raid on the compound.

"Okay," Randall said, pulling out a fist-size camera and focusing on the diagrams on the wall, "get all that shit set out on a desk where I can get some quick pictures. We want to be out of here in half an hour or we'll get our butts caught red-handed."

17

For all their avowed proficiency and power, computers do have limitations and this had been one of those times when the truism had asserted itself.

The major problem was in Kurtzman's search for a breakthrough in the international weapons-dealing operation the Farm had been investigating. It was hard enough for the Bear to effectively broach the security systems protecting domestic intelligence data banks, but to extend his reach to other systems overseas was a quantum leap in terms of logistics.

Kurtzman was having his best success by steering away from intelligence agencies and concentrating on more accessible sources—shipping manifests, cargo inventories, inspection posts. It was a roundabout and definitely more cumbersome way of operating, but he felt sure that in the long run he'd come up with more vital information.

For the next half hour, the entire room was alive with blinking lights and the whirring of tape machines as the complex network of supercomputers acted on Bear's commands, using modems and microwave linkups to sleuth across the continent and abroad for desired information. They also continued to pull in a steady flow of data from the pathology labs working on the body samples from Rayford's Creek.

As he waited, Kurtzman powered his wheelchair over to a filing cabinet and pulled out a thick ream of bound readouts containing all the work he'd done thus far on his walking project. Thumbing through the pages, he kept hoping to come across something that he might have overlooked, some equation or diagram that held the clue to modifying the apparatus. But the breakthrough still eluded him. Maybe if he took up Brognola on the offer for some time off...

His thoughts drifted for a moment and he recalled the days before the shootout that had left him paralyzed. There were the touch football games out on the grounds where the new gymnasium was being erected; hours of jogging at dawn along the scenic vistas of Skyline Drive; forays to the capitol, where he'd always forgone elevators in favor of climbing stairs as a way to keep fit—even if he had to clear more than a dozen floors to make an appointment. The world of the walking... would he ever return to it?

"Maybe," he murmured to himself. "Maybe, someday...."

Behind him, the backup computers had finished their duty and the results were being printed by a space-age laser printer. Kurtzman put his personal file away and returned to the main console. As he looked over the first page of information one particular word drew his attention as it appeared in seven different places.

"All right," he muttered, leaning over and pressing an intercom. "Yo, chief! You around?"

A few seconds later Brognola's voice came over the small speaker. "Yeah, Bear. Got something?"

"You bet. Come on down, and bring some coffee with you."

"I'll be right there."

By the time Brognola reached the computer room, another four pages of data had been churned out by the machines. Brognola picked up one of the sheets and whistled low as he realized Kurtzman's discovery.

"Mountland," he said. "Well, well, what do you know?"

Only last week, during a White House briefing with the heads of various intelligence agencies, the subject of technobanditry had been discussed and preliminary investigations had focused attention on one particular trading firm whose freight ship had run aground in the Mediterranean the week before. Salvage divers had recovered some of the cargo that had spilled into the sea. Customs officials had inspected the goods and found that they were not listed on the ship's manifest. In particular, there were high-tech motherboards and other computer paraphernalia specifically designed for the NORAD installation inside Colorado's Cheyenne Mountain. The ship had belonged to a firm called Interseas Express, but they were making their delivery on behalf of another company—Mountland.

"I think I'll give our boys a quick call on this," Brognola said. "Unless we've missed our guess, we just might have hit the bull's-eye."

PEOPLE WHO'VE NEVER faced misfortune are often astonished to see the apparent ease with which those undergoing great personal trauma can sometimes go about their daily business. But the grieving and wounded often get through the day more easily by focusing on something other than the pain.

So it was with Pamela. Her closest relative had just been buried and she herself had withstood several attempts on her life, the latest of which had nearly claimed the lives of those now with her in the isolated ranger's cabin. And yet, here she was, sitting before her moviola, fussing meticulously over the last bits of footage for her film as if that were her only care in the world. She looked tired but was filled with enough stamina to see the task through. Schwarz and Kissinger were lending what technical expertise they could, helping with sound dubs and splicing, while Blancanales's role was to keep everyone's spirits up.

"I almost feel like a producer," he said, pacing the room. "Only if I was, I'd have a better office than this."

"Yeah," Kissinger wisecracked, "not many places to do lunch out here in the Rockies."

"You're right. And no photo opportunities."

Pamela pushed her chair back and rubbed her eyes as she let out a cleansing sigh.

"Going to make it?" Schwarz asked her.

Pamela checked the clock. "Maybe so," she said. "Maybe so."

"Anything else we can do to speed things up?" Pol asked.

The woman shook her head. "No, no. You've done so much already. I can't believe you risked your necks like that . . . and that you're joking so soon after you were nearly killed."

"Hey, that's our motto," Blancanales chuckled. "A brush with death each day keeps the doldrums away."

They fell silent a moment as they heard the telltale drone of a helicopter. Kissinger broke away from the splicing machine and checked the window.

"It's okay," he said, recognizing Grimaldi behind the controls of the Bell chopper setting down on a cleared patch of flatland near the cabin. Lyons and Lao Ti were riding with him, both having been treated for the wounds they had sustained in the earlier shootout in the ravine near the cemetery.

"Back and at 'em?" Kissinger queried as the others came through the door and immediately headed for the warmth of the fireplace.

"Natch," Lyons said, rubbing his hands over the flames. "We also compared notes with the boys from the Bureau and a few company spooks. Those snipers were definitely Levdroko's people. Got them linked to seven different West Coast hits last year alone. He probably called in a few markers to get them in here."

"Maybe he called in their markers," Blancanales said, "but we cashed in their chips."

"That's not all," Lao Ti added. "When we were flying in we got a call from the Farm. Looks like the red flag's gone up on a place called Mountland Inc. From all early indications they might be the KGB link to this Third World gun-running operation."

"They're based around here?"

Lao Ti nodded. "Got some addresses of all their plants and business offices. The authorities are drawing up warrants, but it looks like there might be a few gray areas they'll want the Team to move around."

"Fine with us," Schwarz said.

"If you need to get moving on it, I've got a handle on this film," Pamela told them.

"I can stay with you," Lao Ti volunteered. "The chopper only holds five, anyway."

"Fair enough," Lyons said, taking charge. He had brought a pack in with him and he withdrew a set of maps, laying them out on the table. "We'll split up and decide who's going to hit where and—"

The communicator in Lyons's pack came to life, giving off a signal indicating that Kurtzman was trying to patch through. Lyons grabbed the device and made the connection.

"Got something new, Bear?"

"Sure do," Kurtzman's voice reported. "Finally got the genetic imprint on those samples you got us."

"Yeah? Who was the stiff?"

"A guy named Chuck Cosvie."

"Hmm," Lyons said. "Doesn't ring a bell."

"Probably shouldn't, at least not yet. He used to be on the board for an outfit called Denver Technological. Used to be a big defense subcontractor—weapon systems and stuff like that. They put out a few clunkers and fell on hard times, so—"

Kissinger, who could hear the conversation, jumped in. "You saying he's linked up with Levdroko?"

"Seems like a sure bet," Bear said. "You see, the official story fed out on Cosvie was that he supposedly embezzled funds and split the country. DTI had a board meeting a couple of days ago and without Cosvie's vote they were able to push through a merger that links them with our KGB conduit."

"Mountland?" Lyons guessed.

"Bingo," Kurtzman said.

18

More than a century ago, General William Palmer set out to create the Rocky Mountains' answer to the grandiose mansion community of Newport, Rhode Island. He ran his Denver & Rio Grande Railroad through a poor miners' town called Colorado City and set about transforming the land on the other side of the tracks into his dream. Over a ten-year period there was frenetic building, with so many Tudor-style mansions shooting up that people off-handedly referred to the area as Little London, even after it had been rechristened Colorado Springs.

In the intervening years, as the city grew, the wealthy began to migrate to the outskirts of town, settling into larger mansions on larger estates. Much of Little London declined in stature, and certain neighborhoods were given over to those people of far lesser means. When baby boomers were crowding the local universities during the sixties and seventies, many of the old mansions were bought up by landlords and quickly subdivided into separate apartments. The state of disrepair quickly increased, especially in buildings used as fraternities.

Gibson Avenue was a textbook example of such real estate de-evolution. Prior to World War I, the street had housed the highest per capita concentration of wealth west of the Mississippi, but now it was unofficially known as University Row. Both Colorado Springs State College and the Denver Trade School had been built nearby. Students were crammed into multistory homes, living out of converted bedrooms. Most exteriors were in dire need of fresh paint and parking was a nightmare. Vehicles choked the curbs and spilled over onto once-manicured lawns. On the weekend, the setting was even further removed from the days of aristocratic gentility. Raucous music poured out of open windows as revelers celebrated Friday night with the usual glut of parties, some of which spilled out onto the street. There was drunken howling and the off-key singing of team fight songs, the plastic clatter of Frisbees skidding across asphalt streets, ant the blare of horns from those attempting to drive through the weekend snarl.

However, chaotic as things were on Gibson Avenue, it was nothing compared to the scene on Gibson Place, a narrow, thirty-yard-long cul-de-sac veering off at the end of the street. There were only four houses on that strip, and two of them had been condemned. The other two served as a boarding house and headquarters for the Heathens motorcycle gang. And if the collegiate revelry down the block was considered some form of societal purgatory, a Heathen Friday night beer bash was the equivalent of hell on earth.

Randall pulled his motorcycle up onto the weed-choked lawn, inching past the other choppers and around a rowdy crowd that encircled two bikers who were struggling to get through a fistfight although both were so drunk they could barely stand. One of the men finally managed to land a sucker punch that doubled over his foe.

Erica had ridden to the party with Randall, and she quickly dismounted the bike as soon as the engine stopped. She was wearing dark mascara and even more makeup than usual. The makeup was not out of any desire to impress the Heathens, but to camouflage the bruises and black eye Randall had given her when he'd finally found her at the apartment earlier. He'd barged in despite her attempt to keep him out, and the ensuing fight had drawn the landlord to their door with threats to call the police. They'd calmed down and, for reasons Erica was still at a loss to understand, she and Randall had somehow called a truce long enough to share the last of her cocaine. The lull of the drug had made it even easier for them to put the fight behind them and move to the bedroom, their most compatible turf.

Now, three hours later, Erica's doubts were flooding back. This was the first time she'd been to Gibson Place, and although she knew how to party, this orgy went far beyond anything she'd ever seen, much less participated in. As another fight broke out on the lawn, she followed Randall up the sidewalk toward the decrepit mansion. Off to her right, she could see several couples rolling about on the grass, half-undressed and noisily mounting one another with no concern or regard for whoever might be watching. There was certainly nothing erotic about it.

"All right, Danny!" Randall called out, recognizing the lock picker as one of the men making out. "Go for it, dude!"

"Yo, Randy!" Danny called out. "Come on over and bring that hot mamma along with you!"

"Gotta see the man first," Randall said. "Maybe later."

Erica felt Randall's hand sliding down her hip and pulling at the hem of her leather miniskirt as he winked at Danny. She wriggled away from him and shot him an angry glance. "Guess again," she snapped at him. "No way am I getting shoved into some group grope!"

Randall grinned at her. "I thought you liked to party!"

"You call that a party?"

Randall shrugged. "Hey, don't knock it till you try it."

They continued up the walk, squeezing past four husky Heathens serving as bouncers. They recognized Randall and let him pass. Erica followed, feeling their lascivious gazes on her.

The inside of the mansion was even more trashed than the grounds. There were countless fist-size holes in the plaster and most of the railing uprights had been kicked out to the point that the bannister of the once-lavish staircase was almost ready to collapse. Bullet holes scarred the ceiling of the main room and several of the windows were boarded up with wood or card-board. The air was thick with smoke and stank with mildew and marijuana.

Erica watched as two bikers tied bandannas tightly around their upper arm and injected each other with heroin from the same syringe. One of them glanced up at her and smiled dully, his eyes glazed and several of his teeth missing from street fights.

There were more than thirty people crowded into the main room, talking loudly above the blare of the stereo and the rumble of motorcycles just outside the front window. Most of the men and a couple of the women wore the Heathen colors. Two huge stainless-steel beer kegs rested on a counter by the staircase, and one of the bikers was busy filling cup after cup of foaming beer to pass around to the party-goers who hadn't brought their own. Randall reached into his hip pocket for a half-pint flask of Scotch and took a long swallow before handing it to Erica. She took a smaller sip, determined that she wasn't going to get herself drunk or drugged to the point where she'd find her-self doing things against her better judgment.

Randall looked around and spotted José in a far corner of the room, drinking from a quart bottle of Wild Turkey as he grimaced and endured the pinprick stabbings of a tattoo artist covering his biceps with the gang's insignia.

"Hey, what it is?" José called out as he spotted Randall approaching him.

"Need to see Syracuse about the plans," Randall said.

"Right," José said. "Ouch! Hey, man, lighten up!" he told the ponytailed man with the tattoo needle.

"Shut up and take another drink," the artist said, laughing. He glanced at Erica and raised an eyebrow. "Nice ass, lady. A butterfly would look real sweet there."

"Forget it," Erica told him. "I've already got a heart."

"Oh? Let me see."

"Go to hell."

The artist looked at Randall. "Hey, man, teach her a few manners, huh?"

"Never mind that," Randall said. "Where's Syracuse?"

"Next door," José said. "You know the code word?"

Randall nodded. He turned to Erica. "Wait here. I'll be back in a few."

"What?"

"You heard me," Randall told her. "I got business to tend to. Make yourself at home."

"Yeah, right...."

Randall grabbed Erica roughly by the elbow and dragged her away from José. Once he'd guided her into the nearest hallway, he pressed her against the wall and leaned his face close to hers.

"You blow my big chance here and what happened earlier's gonna seem like a picnic," he threatened. "Is that clear?"

Erica felt a rush of fear as she looked into Randall's eyes. She'd seen his rage countless times before, but never had their been this much intensity to his gaze. She nodded meekly.

"I didn't hear that!"

"Yes," she murmured. "I understand."

"Good." Randall let go of the woman and stepped back. His features softened and he smiled again. "Then kick back and take it easy awhile."

She nodded a second time. "Okay, Randall. Sure."

"That's more like it!" He gave her a thumbs-up, then turned and wove his way through the crowd until he was back outside.

Erica stayed in the hallway, trying to avoid the mob packed into the main room. A door opened behind her and she saw another biker coming out from one of the side rooms, sheathing a bowie knife as he hitched up his pants. He eyed Erica a moment, then walked silently past her and headed for the nearest keg. Erica looked back at the side room, peering past the partly opened door and seeing a girl slowly putting on her clothes. Tears were streaming down her face and she was sobbing uncontrollably.

"That does it," Erica muttered to herself. Drawing in a deep breath, she headed back into the crowd, fending off several advances on her way to the front door. Once back outside, she cut across the lawn and took long strides until she was back on Gibson Avenue. Leaving the Heathens behind, she started down University Row, watching the college students going about their revelry with an exaggerated sense of doing the forbidden.

"You poor shits," she muttered to no one in particular. "If you only knew..."

THE HOUSE NEXT DOOR to the Heathens' party was surrounded by an eight-foot-high brick wall covered with a thick layer of ivy. There was a wrought-iron gate adjacent to the driveway, and when Randall reached it after inching past yet another fistfight, he found his way barred by a huge Heathen, appropriately named Kong. Standing six foot seven and weighing well over 340 pounds, the man was leaning against the gate with his tattooed arms folded across his chest and a bored expression on his mustached face.

"Party's the other way, punk," he told Randall.

"I'm here to do the Syracuse shuffle," Randall said calmly as he paused to light a cigarette.

Kong took a closer look at Randall, then stepped aside and grunted as he pulled open the gate and motioned him inside.

Randall strode across the driveway to the side entrance of the second mansion. In sharp contrast to the wild pandemonium next door, this estate was deathly quiet. Although a porch lamp glowed dimly, there were no lights on inside. Looming up against the night, the house looked like something out of a horror movie. It was the kind of place where hapless newlyweds sought refuge on stormy nights, never to be seen or heard from again. Randall shuddered involuntarily as he started up the steps. For the first time he was beginning to have his doubts about what he was getting into. He was certainly no naive innocent—he'd killed and had taken part in more than his share of debauchery, after all—but now he suddenly wondered if he was taking a dangerously long and irreversible step.

He hesitated on the porch as he finished his cigarette, debating whether or not to go through with everything. It was possible that he could sneak up the driveway and scale the gateway there . . . or was it? He heard a growling off in the distance and could make out the faint outline of a German shepherd pacing back and forth before the gate, tethered by a twenty-foot length of chain.

There was a sudden rustling above his head and Randall took a reflexive step backward, glancing up to see a foot-long rat scurry across a beam above the doorway. As quickly as it had appeared, the rat vanished into the shadows. Randall let out his breath and dropped his cigarette on the concrete. As he was stubbing it out, someone stepped out into view to his right.

"You taking a leak here or what?"

Randall glanced over and saw Syracuse looking up at him from the grounds. The gangleader motioned him down from the steps. "Through the storm cellar," he said.

Randall joined Syracuse and they walked along the side of the house where two ancient wooden doors had been pulled open to reveal a cement staircase leading down to the mansion's basement.

"Just rounding up the artillery," Syracuse explained as he drummed his knuckles on the reinforced steel door at the base of the steps. Moments later the door was pulled open by another member of the Heathens, and Randall was led into the cellar.

After being out in the dark for so long, the sudden burst of light within the subterranean chamber was almost blinding. Once his pupils adjusted, Randall saw that the basement was filled with an arsenal of weapons that would have made a SWAT team proud. Assault rifles, semiautomatics, grenades, plastic explosives...the Heathens had it all.

"Shit," Randall muttered in disbelief. "Where'd you get all this?"

"Went trick-or-treating," Syracuse wisecracked. From the warning look on the man's face, Randall guessed that was the closest he'd get to a straight answer. He'd heard Danny and José boast about robbing a few gun shops and cutting some kind of deal with a procurement officer with the Air Force, trading heroin and cocaine for weapons. However they'd gotten their hands on it, the arsenal was certainly adequate enough for staging the kind of siege the Heathens had in mind.

Vast as the supply of weaponry was, it took up only a small corner of the large basement. The rest of the room was filled with cots, two huge wire cages stocked with bricks of marijuana and the equipment necessary for cutting cocaine and heroin before putting it out on the streets. There was also a large, scarred table where a dozen men Randall hadn't seen at the party were examining a series of maps depicting Buck Howser's secret installation in the mountains.

"Brought in some outside help," Syracuse explained, referring to the other men. "Thought we could use some ex-grunts who pulled a little guerrilla duty during Nam. When we hit this place, we want to hit it hard and do it right. Anybody gets in our way, they're dead meat."

Randall stared numbly at the other men as a second, even more odious realization finally dawned on him. He was helping to plan, not only the raiding of Buck Howser's hole in the hills, but possibly the murder of his father, as well. In moments of anger he'd often thought of killing the old man, but it was always a notion that passed with time, even after the confrontation that had caused Howser to kick him off the property. Now it was different. Now he wasn't just wishing the guy dead—he was putting the plan into motion that would likely ensure that it happened.

"Hey, cheer up, Randy," Syracuse told him, slapping him on the back. "Just think, once we pull this off, you're going to be one of us."

19

The huge semi slowed and carefully negotiated the sharp turn bringing it up to the security gate at Mountland Distribution. The driver leaned out his window and handed the usual papers to a uniformed security guard.

"Where's Jeff?" the guard asked as he scanned the papers and handed them back to the driver.

"Little under the weather tonight," the driver said.

"Knowing Jeff he's probably just hung over." The guard laughed, stepping back and triggering a switch to open the gates.

"Could be," the driver said with a grin. "Could just be."

Once inside the parking lot, the truck made a slow, sharp U-turn, then began backing up to the loading dock of the nearest warehouse.

"Since when have you known how to drive an eighteen-wheeler?" Kissinger asked Grimaldi as he sat on the passenger side of the truck's cab.

"Jets, trucks, what's the difference," Grimaldi snickered as he kept an eye on his rear- and side-view mirrors, easing the truck back with surprising ease for a man who, in fact, hadn't been behind the wheel of a semi for more than seven years.

Kissinger reached for the truck's CB radio and keyed the mike as he brought it to his mouth. "Big Wad to Peashooter," he said cryptically. "We're in."

Another man's voice cracked over the radio speaker. "We're right behind you."

OLEG LEVDROKO DABBED at his forehead with a handkerchief as he left the rest room of Mountland Distribution. He'd just given himself another injection, but the usual quick rush of relief had yet to come over him and he was still fighting off the agony of pain that pounded inside his skull. It had been all he could do to get through Howser's tour of the mine and he'd been relieved when they'd returned from the mountain area and Howser had dropped him off. The tumor was growing, of that much he was certain. How long could he expect to function before he had to finally own up to the illness and take himself out of the arena he loved so much? He hoped he wouldn't have to make that decision. Even more, he hoped that he could reverse the trend of events that had dogged him since he'd come north from New Mexico. The Colorado job was to have capped off his brilliant career. Instead it was turning into a debacle of missed opportunity and bungled execution. Somehow he had to turn it all around.

"You all right, pardner?" General Tom Christie asked when Levdroko joined him and Wild Bill Greason. "I hate to say it, but you look like shit."

"I'll be okay," Levdroko said. "Just something I had for lunch, I think."

"You're sure?"

Levdroko nodded. "Let's get on with this."

"Fine by me," Christie said.

They walked down the back corridor of the warehouse. "I think the truck just came in, so you can have a look at some of the equipment while we're loading," Greason told both men.

The "equipment" Greason was referring to was a shipment of forty-two-dozen half-completed, obsolete missile housings Mountland had manufactured fourteen months ago, prior to announced defense cutbacks in production of midrange warheads. A clause in Mountland's contract allowed the Pentagon to back out of the deal by a certain cutoff date with only a minimal payment forfeiture. When the order to halt production had come in on exactly that date, Greason had to face up to the dismal prospect that a once-lucrative 2.2 million dollar profit had suddenly nose-dived into a seven hundred thousand dollar deficit.

As with the WH-32 rocket launchers, however, Greason had found a way not only to recoup his losses on the black market, but to double the money he would have originally made. By joining forces with Christie's Ryco/Kent scrap operations, Greason had found a low-cost way to finish the production run.

And once the missiles were secreted out to Buck Howser's mountain facility, they would be stored until the DTI/Mountland merger came through and the nuclear-waste disposal contracts were finalized. At that point spent fuel rods would be reprocessed for the plutonium required to make compatible triggers that would turn the supposedly useless missiles into viable nuclear warheads, ready for sale to the Third World.

The main warehouse, roughly the size of a high school gymnasium, was bustling with activity, as Greason had crews working double-time to ship out as much inventory as possible before a rumored sweep of Justice Department-ordered inspections made its way up the central Denver corridor. The WH-32s were already en route to Saint Louis, and if the missile parts could be transferred to Ryco/Kent, the only suspect inventory Greason would have to explain would be a surplus stock of faulty tank treads and power plants for the Wolverine-13 Land Rovers. In both instances there was still some time before they were required to be disposed of.

Levdroko swallowed hard and grimaced at the unrelenting pain inside his head, and as he entered the warehouse he suddenly veered to one side and leaned against a stack of packing skids. A wild flood of small lights flashed before his eyes, then were choked out by a sudden rush of darkness. He began to perspire and his pulse quickened. It was only by force of sheer willpower that he was able to prevent himself from losing consciousness completely.

"Shit, pal," General Christie said, "you must have gotten food poisoning or something. You look like you're dying."

"Tom's right," Greason said. He glanced over at the nearest workers and waved two men over, telling them, "Take Mr. Shearston here to the employees' lounge, then call in an ambulance so—"

"No, no," Levdroko whispered through his pain. "Just take me there and let me lay down a few minutes and I'll be fine." If he could get off by himself for another injection, the extra dose might help him weather this latest episode. The last thing he wanted was to wind up in a hospital, where it would quickly be established that he had morphine in his system and wasn't the man he claimed to be.

"Whatever, man," one of the workers said, jumping into a small cart and gesturing for his partner to get Levdroko into the other seat. "I'll just scoot him over to the lounge."

"Fine," Greason said. He turned to Levdroko, whose face was waxen and ash-colored. "We'll stop by in a few minutes and check on you."

Levdroko nodded faintly and let himself be eased into the cart. Christie opened the main door, giving the worker just enough room to drive the cart through. Once Levdroko was out of their sight, the two generals moved away from the others and spoke to each other in whispers.

"I don't know about this guy," Christie said. "Something ain't right about him."

"Tell me about it," Greason complained. "I didn't much care for him from the first."

"Damn Ruskies anyway," Christie said. "Things were working out just fine with Tewkneda, then they have to call her back and stick us with some basket case."

"Well, as long as the money keeps rolling in, I can live with it, I guess," Greason said. "C'mon, let's make sure this shipment gets out so—"

"Wait!" Christie suddenly interrupted. "Hear that?"

Greason strained his ears, and above the din of activity around him, he was finally able to detect the howl of sirens and the drone of a nearby helicopter. "What the hell?"

Both men headed over to the nearest windows overlooking the parking lot. Six cars bearing the U.S. marshal's insignia were roaring onto the property, rooftop beacons flashing. A bright beam from the overhead chopper shone down on the asphalt.

"I don't believe it!" Greason exclaimed. "It's a bust!"

"Shit!" Christie spat angrily as he recoiled from the window. "I don't need this."

Picking up his stride, he made a beeline for the back loading dock, where workers swarmed around the truck that had just backed up to the warehouse. Greason followed quickly behind him, muttering, "No shit. I don't know what the hell they're pulling, but for now we'd best lie low. I'll get in touch with my lawyers and we'll get off the hook."

CARL LYONS GLANCED at the three Denver Police Special Assignment officers crouched with him inside the back of the semi.

"Sounds like showtime," he said, listening to the clatter on the other side of the door separating them from the warehouse. In addition to the sound of latches being unfastened, they could also make out the wail of sirens and the thunder of the helicopter still hovering above the facility.

All four men were dressed for combat in navy-colored outfits mottled with patches of black and dark brown to allow them to blend in better with the night. They all wore Kevlar bullet-proof vests similar in design to the one that had saved Lao Ti's life during the siege in the mountains. Where Lyons differed most from the other three was in his choice of firearms. The officers relied on standard-issue riot guns and service revolvers, but the Ironman had hauled along his pride and joy, a customized Colt Python. He reflexively swung out the cylinder to check on his ammunition and felt reassured by the presence of the 158-grain hollowpoints nestled in the chambers. He had three speed-loaders packed in his vest on the chance that the siege became more brutal and dragged-out than anticipated.

The workers on the dock were already startled by the sudden arrival of the U.S. marshals and the overhead chopper that continually bathed them in its harsh glow. When they saw Grimaldi and Kissinger yank open the truck doors and let another four gunmen pour out onto the dock, their surprise turned to fear.

One dock worker threw his hands up in the air and began wailing for mercy.

"Hey, man, don't kill me. I got a wife and kids and my mom's in the hospital—"

"Shut up and get out of my way, or you'll be on the bed next to her," Lyons barked as he bolted onto the loading platform and quickly sized up the situation. The marshals were in the process of storming the building's front entrances and the three-man squad with the Ironman was already on its way into the warehouse. No shots had been fired yet, and a major reason for the show of force had been to dissuade anyone from even considering the thought of shooting their way out of the facility. As with any building housing a wealth of armaments, it was a foremost concern to eliminate the possibility of triggering a chain-reaction explosion that would level the site and everything else within a two-block radius.

"Over there!" Grimaldi suddenly cried out, spotting Generals Greason and Christie scrambling for a drab-colored Plymouth parked in the employee lot behind the building.

"We'll get 'em," Kissinger told Lyons.

"Good," Ironman said. "I'll check things out inside."

As Lyons followed the police agents inside, Kissinger and Grimaldi leapt down from the loading dock and broke into runs as they headed for the fleeing Generals. Cowboy drew his weapon and shouted a warning.

"Freeze! Government agents!"

"Freeze my ass," Greason snarled as he opened the driver's door of the Plymouth and slid in behind the wheel. Christie paused outside the car, using it for cover as he pulled out an automatic and drew beads on his pursuers.

Kissinger instinctively dove to his right, rolling behind a Dumpster as bullets clanged off the metal siding. Grimaldi tumbled in the other direction and came up firing from behind a parked Honda Civic. His .45 was moded for 3-shot bursts, and he made each of the shots count. Christie sprang back and fell to the ground as he took a slug to the upper shoulder of his gun hand. The other two shots skimmed off the front windshield, effectively obstructing Greason's vision as he started up the engine and tried to drive off.

Christie howled in agony as the car bounded over his right leg and his gun fell a few yards away from him. As he tried to crawl over to it, Grimaldi dashed forward and kicked the weapon aside, then leveled his own gun at the general's forehead.

"Going somewhere?" Grimaldi inquired as he and Christie found themselves caught in the near-blinding glow of the chopper's searchlight.

Kissinger, meanwhile, realized that the Plymouth had to drive past the Dumpster to make its getaway. He quickly climbed up to the lip of the huge container, leaping out onto the hood of the car as it sped past. Greason was driving with his window open so he could lean out and see where he was going. When he found Kissinger straddling the hood, he used his left hand to reach for a gun from his shoulder holster. Before he could get to the weapon, however, he clipped the edge of the Dumpster and the car spun out of control.

Kissinger felt himself sliding off the hood. Rather than fight the inevitable, he let the laws of physics take over and send him flying to the asphalt. Using the same finely tuned reflexes that had served him so well on the gridiron half a lifetime ago, he rolled and narrowly averted being crushed by the Plymouth, which popped a tire against the sharp corner of a concrete parking curb and did a roll of its own.

When the vehicle came to an upside-down landing, a stunned Greason struggled to crawl out, smelling the warning fumes of a gas leak. He was halfway out when a spark ignited the fumes inside the engine compartment. There was a resounding explosion that ripped the car in two, in the process turning General Greason into a charred and mutilated travesty of his former self. Engulfed by flames, one arm blown clear off his torso, the man screamed one last cry before death silenced him forever.

Kissinger hurriedly rose to his feet and tracked down a firehose mounted to the side of the building. A new siren contributed to the night's din as he broke the safety glass and dragged the hose toward the burning wreckage. Grimaldi passed him on the way and went back to the wall, cranking up the water pressure so that Kissinger could direct the spray at the car in hopes of keeping the flames from spreading to the nearby building. Several U.S. marshals had arrived to take General Christie into custody.

WHILE THE WAREHOUSE WORKERS were herded together and the authorities began the time-consuming task of checking the inventory and books for evidence of criminal activity, Lyons prowled the back corridors, Python in hand, looking for anyone who might have fled for cover during the initial stage of the siege.

Halfway down the ground-floor hallway, he came to a stop, seeing a man sprawled face down on the floor next to a small transport cart. Lyons crouched beside the man briefly and felt for a pulse. He was still alive and there was a large raised welt on the back of his head where he'd obviously been struck with a blunt instrument.

Alert to possible danger, Lyons glanced up and down the hallway. Ten feet ahead was the research-and-development lab, with posted warnings advising that only those with top-level security passes would be granted admittance. The door, however, was unguarded and partially ajar. Rising from his crouch, Lyons warily approached the entrance and eased the door open.

Inside was a vacant antechamber with a secretarial station and numerous file cabinets. There was an inner window that looked out on the main laboratory, and when Lyons looked through the glass he suddenly froze.

A vaguely familiar figure was hunched over one of the workbenches, toying with what looked like the warhead for a TOW missile. Every few seconds the man would look away from his work and grimace in pain.

Lyons inched to the inner doorway and eased his way into the lab, raising his Python into firing position.

"End of the line, Levdroko," the Ironman said with calm authority.

Levdroko glanced up at Lyons. His eyes had a wild gleam and sweat rolled down his forehead. He smiled. "What an appropriate choice of words."

"Get away from the table."

Levdroko shook his head. "I'm a dying man," he confided. "There's nothing you can do to hurt me."

"Get away from the table," Lyons repeated. "And get your hands off that contraption."

"On, it's more than a contraption," Levdroko assured the other man. "See this switch my finger's on? One little touch the wrong way and they'll think someone dropped the bomb on Denver. Who knows how many people would die? Hundreds? Thousands? More?"

"You wouldn't do that," Lyons said.

"Oh?" Levdroko smiled. "What makes you so sure?"

"For starters, you'd be the first one to buy it."

"But I just told you I'm a dying man." As if to support his contention, Levdroko shook slightly, riding out the throes of pain inside his skull. "At least this way, I can die famous. Your American newspapers love to print long stories about your greatest murderers. I could outshine all the others with one flick of the switch."

"It doesn't take much talent to flick a switch, Levdroko."

"Put your gun down," the Russian commanded, suddenly moving away from the table and holding the warhead cradled in one arm like a small infant. "Now!"

Lyons hesitated a moment, trying to weigh the odds. He decided it was too risky to play hardball at this point. Levdroko was obviously disturbed and one of the first things Lyons had learned during his days with the LAPD was that one doesn't reason with a madman, because the mad respond to their own twisted logic and any attempt to counter that only complicates matters. On the other hand, he'd also learned during those police days that a good officer never turned his gun over to the enemy, no matter what the circumstances.

As a compromise, Lyons lowered the Colt to his side and stared at Levdroko, trying to gauge his next move.

"I'm sure you're no stranger to pain," Levdroko said, gritting his teeth as he spoke. His voice took on a high-pitched, strained tone and tears began to well in his eyes. "Even the worst pain you've ever experienced is nothing compared to what I'm feeling right now."

"Give yourself up and you can get help," Lyons calmly suggested.

Levdroko laughed. "There's nothing to be done! It can't be operated on."

"What?"

"The tumor!" Levdroko screamed. "The tumor!"

With his free hand, the Russian suddenly reached inside his coat and pulled out a small palm-size .22. He put the gun to his head and grinned at Lyons.

"Levdroko, don't..."

Lyons lunged forward, but before he could intervene, Levdroko squeezed the trigger. As the bullet smashed through his skull, ending his pain, Levdroko jerked in place and lost his grip on the warhead.

Diving forward, Lyons grabbed the falling piece of weaponry like a wide receiver hauling in a long pass. He pulled it in close to his chest as he hit the floor, bracing himself for what he thought would be an explosion that would send him to a deep and final grave. The warhead didn't go off, however, and as he slowly climbed back to his feet, Lyons realized that half the components were missing. Levdroko had been bluffing all along.

Glancing to the floor, Lyons saw the Russian twisted grotesquely in his own blood. His eyes were open but there was no life in them.

"Tough break, Levdroko," Lyons muttered as he hoisted his Python. "You should have quit while you were ahead."

IT WASN'T JUST RANDALL.

Erica had had enough of Colorado, period. She wasn't sure who she'd been fooling besides herself, but after her eye-opening venture through the living hell of the Heathens' beer blast, she knew that she'd taken a wrong turn with her life a long time ago. Luckily she had a chance to make another start, and she was going to see to it that Randall paid for how he had treated her.

"Dirtbag," she muttered contemptuously under her breath as she piled one last load of possessions from her apartment into the back of Randall's pickup. She had paid her rent a few weeks in advance, but at this point she was willing to write that money off, along with her security deposit. Once she was finished clearing out, she figured she'd make a quick stop at the corner minimal for some road provisions, then she was going to fill the truck with gas and get on the highway. She planned to drive southwest until she finally made her way to Los Angeles, where she had some friends who would put her up and help forge the necessary papers to put the truck in her name. Erica figured it was a small price for him to pay considering all the misery he'd heaped on her during their tumultuous relationship.

It was past two-thirty in the morning and the parking lot was quiet as she climbed in behind the wheel and started the engine. Shifting the pickup into reverse, she was about to back up when she suddenly slammed on the brakes.

"What the hell?" she exclaimed, seeing that another car had braked to a stop directly behind her, blocking her way. The doors of the other vehicle swung open and two men hurriedly scrambled out. One stood near the back of the pickup while the other rushed to her window, pulling a badge from his coat, along with a menacing-looking .45 automatic.

"Turn off the engine, please, ma'am," Pol Blancanales asked the woman calmly.

Erica drew in a deep breath, trying not to lose her cool. "What's this all about?" she asked calmly as she switched off the ignition and glanced at the I.D. "I haven't done anything..."

"This vehicle belongs to one Randall Howser," Blancanales said, passing along information Kurtzman had finally managed to pull from his computers. "We're kind of anxious to talk to him."

"He's not here," Erica said, thinking fast, trying to weigh her options.

"Any idea where he is?" Blancanales asked. On a hunch, he acted on another piece of information the Bear had provided after running a check on the tattoo image that had turned up on the freeze-frame blowup from Pamela's movie. "He wouldn't be hanging out somewhere with the Heathens, would he?"

Erica looked at Blancanales and realized there was no use lying, and no reason to, either. "Yeah," she muttered, "he's with them, all right. But they've got something planned way out of town, so I don't know if you're going to be able to find him.''

Blancanales smiled thinly at the woman. ''Try us,'' he said.

20

The first hint of dawn was creeping above the eastern horizon, but there was still adequate cover for the large panel truck rolling its way through the mountains. Stenciled lettering on the side of the truck suggested that the driver was hauling product on behalf of Carlyle Furniture but, like the semi that had helped the authorities make their raid on the Mountland Distribution warehouse, the vehicle was packed with human cargo. The battle-scarred war vets that Syracuse had brought in for the raid on Buck Howser's mountain compound were huddled in the dark enclosure, clutching weapons they were experienced at using and ready to use again. None of them spoke above the drone of the truck's engine and the rattling of its chassis as the vehicle made its way over the uneven road. In a few minutes they knew that the truck would pull off on the shoulder and they would pile out, using the heavy-duty bolt cutters to get past the weakest link in the compound's vast border. Once onto the private property, the men would break into small groups and steal across the terrain to their rendezvous point near the mouth of the old gold mine that now housed Howser's arsenal and facilities for the manufacturing of nuclear weapons. No matter how much of an element of surprise they had, they knew full well that some of their group would not survive the siege. They all had hard-edged memories of friends who had been cut down in the jungles of Southeast Asia.

Randall was riding up front with Syracuse and José, who was behind the wheel.

"Nice truck for a freebie, eh?" José boasted as he guided the vehicle around another tight turn, downshifting as he eased off on the accelerator.

"Yeah," Randall muttered. He was tense and the gun tucked inside the waistband of his jeans made him feel even more uncomfortable as it dug into his pelvis. Like the others, he'd stopped drinking hours before and switched over to speed and cocaine to at least maintain a semblance of alertness. Beneath the rush of chemical stimulation, however, he could feel fatigue gnawing at his nerves. He was hungry, too, even if his stomach was so knotted he doubted that he could keep anything down.

"Hey, lighten up, Rand-Aid," Syracuse joked, giving Howser a light jab in the ribs. "The grunts'll take most of the heat. We'll just hang back and root 'em on, maybe pick off a few sentries along the way."

"Quit poking me, damn it!" Randall snapped.

Syracuse clucked his tongue and shook his head calmly, then without warning, he whipped out his .357 Magnum and pressed the barrel against Randall's cheek. "Just who the shit do you think you're talking to?" he demanded.

Randall swallowed hard but said nothing, feeling the cold metal against his skin. He cursed himself for having gotten into this situation. How could he have ever thought he wanted to deal with the likes of the Heathens? Shit, if there was only some way he could take it all back.

"Y'know what, José?" Syracuse called out as he shoved his gun farther into Randall's face. "I think maybe old Rand's got the shakes 'cause he's holding something back on us. Whaddya think?"

"Nah," José said. "Give the guy a break."

Syracuse looked hard at Randall. "It had better just be nerves...or have you got us headed into some kind of trap."

"No," Randall whispered hoarsely. "No trap."

"Well, I tell you what," Syracuse said, slowly pulling the gun away. "Just so we can be sure you aren't bullshitting us, I changed my mind about you hanging back. I think maybe you oughta lead the charge on the mine, okay?"

Randall felt a pronounced shudder of fear slam its way through his chest. Before he could say anything, however, José suddenly slammed on the brakes and shouted, "What the hell...!"

Directly ahead, a Bell helicopter had suddenly dropped into view and landed in the middle of the road. Two men quickly tumbled out of the chopper, each cradling an M-16 in their arms and spraying lead against the front end of the truck. Tires burst and the engine died as bullets bit into their target.

"I was right!" Syracuse shouted with rage. He slammed his Magnum back into Randall's ribs and pulled the trigger once, blasting a lethal hole in his chest. "Die!"

Randall was already dead, and as he slumped forward, smacking his head off the dashboard, Syracuse squirmed away from him and swung open the passenger door of the cab. He used it for a shield as he took aim at the men who had piled out of the chopper.

John Kissinger and Carl Lyons both dived clear of the road and used the surrounding rocks for cover as they prepared for the shoot-out. Grimaldi, who had taken over the controls of the chopper from the U.S. marshal who'd turned the aircraft over to Able Team back at the Mountland warehouse, lifted off again and circled around the back of the truck. He touched down so close to the back doors of the truck that when the vets inside tried to open them, the rotorwash made it next to impossible. Even when they did manage to inch the door open, there was a loud clang of metal against metal as the rotor slapped against it, effectively pinning them inside.

Lyons and Kissinger had little trouble outmatching José and Syracuse. The truck driver had gotten off only a couple of shots with the Mini-Uzi he'd pulled out from under his seat, but all his bullets had skimmed off the rocks. Cowboy's return fire, however, had stitched José across the upper chest and throat, staining the inside cab with bright jets of blood from a ruptured carotid artery.

Syracuse was a surprisingly good shot, and although he managed to keep Lyons pinned down long enough to give himself a chance for freedom, the gang leader had only managed to scramble a few dozen yards down a steep embankment before Lyons was back onto him.

"Freeze!" Lyons shouted down at the man as he leveled the M-16 at him.

But Syracuse kept running, pausing only long enough to fire wildly over his shoulder. Lyon's rifle rattled in the Ironman's firm grip and seconds later Syracuse was tumbling off balance to the bottom of the shallow ravine, coming to a final rest at the edge of a small stream that trickled innocently past in the dawn's early light.

Lyons and Kissinger both moved around to the back of the truck, each of them grabbing at their waists for an Army-issue gas mask, which they quickly pulled over their heads. Lyons had a tear-gas grenade, and the moment Grimaldi pulled the chopper up and away from the truck doors, he pulled the pin and let fly with the weapon. It landed just below the base of the truck and exploded with a massive cloud of noxious gas that immediately seeped inside the truck as the grunt force pushed the doors open. Half-blinded and overcome by the fumes, the men put up only the slightest resistance before a set of warning blasts from the two

M-16s was followed by a command given by Lyons for them to drop their guns and throw up their hands.

"Good job, Ironman," Kissinger told Lyons as they watched the tormented commandos spill out of the truck, gagging and coughing for fresh air. Grimaldi was touching down again, and overhead another five choppers thundered into view, all of them larger Hueys summoned after a quick call to the Air Force by Hal Brognola. One of the aircraft angled down for a landing on the road, dispatching backup forces to contend with the would-be marauders. The other four choppers continued droning their way farther into the mountain country, bound for the mountain enclave where they would touch down and discharge enough well-armed men to effectively seize control of Buck Howser's facility.

"Sorry to spoil your panty-raid, guys, " Lyons jeered at the grunts.

BUCK HOWSER SNAPPED OFF the shortwave radio and sat silently a moment, numb with shock and rage. How could it all have crumbled so fast? So many years in preparation, so many shrewd maneuvers, so many secret arrangements...everything calculated specifically to avoid the kind of mistakes that befall enterprises that are spawned in a state of reckless fervor. He'd manipulated scores of people, balanced relations between friends and foes alike to ensure the loyalty of both groups.

And now, in a matter of a few short hours, it had come undone.

First he'd heard of the raid at the Mountland warehouse and the loss of Greason, Christie and that bastard Levdroko. That alone would have been cause enough for despair. But that had only been the beginning. Now there was word from the compound in the mountains. Four Hueys headed directly for the installation. An intercepted radio message telling of a shoot-out on the access road that had resulted in the deaths of several armed members of a motorcycle club...including Randall Howser.

"Damn you," Buck cursed his son, erroneously blaming him for all that had happened. "I'll get through all this, just so I can spit on your grave."

He was in the basement war room of his home. Moving away from the radio set, he patiently opened a wall safe, pulling out a soft leather satchel containing over two million dollars worth of uncut diamonds, negotiable bonds, securities and unmarked cash. He'd had such a nest egg set aside for years, in the unlikely event that circumstances such as this would necessitate a quick and long-term getaway. His passport was in the bag, as well, and after making a call to South Am Airlines, he was prepared to live out the scenario he'd pinned on Chuck Cosvie less than a week ago. He would fly to Argentina, then quickly backtrack to Peru, where he had a small but isolated coastal retreat that he'd bought five years before under an assumed name. He could lie low there and plot his next move. This one dream was shattered, but dreams for Buck Howser were plentiful. He'd just start over.

Howser already had a pistol in his shoulder harness. As an added precaution, he opened his gun case and took out the Ingram submachine gun. There were various ways for a man of his distinction and persuasion to get such weapons aboard an aircraft, and there was another cache of firearms down in Peru.

Emerging from the basement, the general heard his rottweilers howling out in the yard. Swearing under his breath, he unlatched the safety on the Ingram and headed for the nearest window. Glancing out, he saw the reason for the barking. A terrified raccoon was being held at bay in the sycamore just outside the kitchen window. The masked creature clung to one of the lower boughs and stared down at the barking dogs that circled the tree, jaws snapping with each howl.

Lowering the Ingram, Howser opened the back door and stepped out onto the patio, shouting, "Ten hut!"

The dogs immediately fell silent and backed away from the tree, squatting on their haunches as they eyed their master. Howser calmly raised his Ingram and was about to nail the raccoon with a horizontal rain of parabellum when he heard a voice behind him.

"Another couple of weeks till hunting season, Bucky," Blancanales called out. "Leave the poor critter alone."

Howser whirled and saw Blancanales perched atop the porch roof, peering around the upper end of a stone chimney. Without waiting for explanation, Howser swung the Ingram around and brought it up firing. Blancanales leaned away from the line of fire and bullets chipped away at the stonework.

"Save some for me!" Gadgets Schwarz called out from the rooftop of the adjacent garage, where he lay prone next to the wire cage that had contained the raccoon they'd used to lure Howser outside.

The general spun around and tried to get off another round of shots, but Schwarz had the drop on him. His .45 was clicked into 3-shot mode, and the death blasts lived up to their name, slamming into Howser with lethal force, obliterating flesh and bone as they sought his heart. For a moment the general had a look of indignant fury, but then the life dropped from his gaze and he crumpled to the ground. The rottweilers whined, not sure what to make of it.

Blancanales emerged from behind the chimney and glanced across the rooftop to Schwarz.

"You all right?" Gadgets asked him.

"Yeah," Blancanales muttered, staring down at the corpse of the slain general. "I'm a lot better than he is, that's for sure."

"Amen," Schwarz said. "Looks like another one bites the dust."

EPILOGUE

"Honorable mention's nothing to turn your nose up at," Blancanales told Pamela as they left the auditorium where the film festival had been held.

"I know," Pamela conceded. "Given all that happened, just getting it finished and entered on time was a miracle. To have actually won a prize was, well, it only made it that much more special."

The others had also attended the festival and filed out of the auditorium behind them. Lyons caught up to Pamela. "I swear, seeing your uncle up there on the screen after hearing so much about him, it's almost like I knew him personally. Seems like he was a swell guy," the Ironman said.

"One of the best," Pol agreed. "He'll be missed."

"But not forgotten," Schwarz said, telling Pamela, "Didn't I hear that guy from the mining company say they wanted to cover all the expenses for the film and buy copies for their film library."

Pamela nodded, blushing modestly. "Yeah, and he also said he's got a friend in the film department at UCLA. Who knows, a couple of months from now I might be back in Los Angeles."

"Well, wherever you end up, I'm sure you'll do well," Lao Ti said.

On the way to the parking lot they passed a newspaper rack, and the daily paper was filled with front page stories about the joint busts at Mountland Distribution and Buck Howser's military installation in the mountains. As was usually the case when Able Team lent its special support to a sensitive operation, they were mentioned nowhere in any of the articles and had to take a private pride in their accomplishment.

"One of our tougher ones," Grimaldi commented.

John Kissinger chuckled to himself as he unlocked the door to one of the rental cars they would be taking out to the airport. "They never seem to get any easier, do they?"

"Knowing us," Lyons wisecracked, "as soon as they did get easier we'd all hang it up."

"Right on," Pol said. "As long as they keep coming at us with their best shot, we're going to stay hard and live large. That's what it's all about, isn't it?"

"You bet," Lyons said. "You bet...."

**A different world—
a different war**

JAMES AXLER

Red Equinox

Ryan Cawdor and his band of postnuclear survivors enter
a malfunctioning gateway and are transported to Moscow,
where Americans are hated with an almost religious fervor
and blamed for the destruction of the world.

**Nile Barrabas's most daring mission is
about to begin . . .**

THE BARRABAS BLITZ

JACK HILD

*An explosive situation is turned over to a crack
commando squad led by Nile Barrabas when a
fanatical organization jeopardizes the NATO alliance
by fueling public unrest and implicating the United
States and Russia in a series of chemical spills.*

More than action adventure...
books written by the men who were there

VIETNAM: GROUND ZERO T.M.

ERIC HELM

Told through the eyes of an American Special Forces squad, an
elite jungle fighting group of strike-and-hide specialists fight a
dirty war half a world away from home.

These books cut close to the bone, telling it the way it
really was.

"Vietnam at Ground Zero is where this book is
written. The author has been there, and he knows.
I salute him and I recommend this book to my
friends."
>   —Don Pendleton
>   creator of *The Executioner*

"Helm writes in an evocative style that gives us Nam as
it most likely was, without prettying up or undue
bitterness."
>   —*Cedar Rapids Gazette*

"Eric Helm's Vietnam series embodies a literary
standard of excellence. These books linger in the
mind long after their reading."
>   —*Midwest Book Review*

Available wherever paperbacks are sold.

**Phoenix Force—bonded in secrecy to avenge the acts
of terrorists everywhere.**

Super Phoenix Force #2

American ''killer'' mercenaries are involved in a KGB plot to
overthrow the government of a South Pacific island. The American President, anxious to preserve his country's image and not
disturb the precarious position of the island nation's government, sends in the experts—Phoenix Force—to prevent a coup.